Dead at the take-off

"They're trying to kill me," Maria screamed. She unhooked her seat belt and crouched on the floor. *What about me? God damn it!*

I ignored her. The flaming wreckage swerved to the right, coming towards my plane. I couldn't stop in time. I didn't want to. Two men with pistols came running our way.

I released the brakes and pushed the throttle all the way in. I had to pass the wreck and get airborne.

Slowly, slowly the airspeed needle crept towards the green arrow. The Seneca was still moving towards my path. My engine's RPMs approached red line. I didn't care. Still not fast enough. Maria screamed something in Spanish. She held her crucifix to her lips.

Dan Goldberg's marriage is already in jeopardy because of his aluminum mistress, a 30-year-old single-engine Cessna. He barely affords the plane by taking extra work teaching monthly statistics classes in Washington D.C. On this trip, everything takes a decidedly different turn when he meets Maria, a sexy Latin businesswoman — and his life shifts.

BOLD VENTURE

FLYING BLIND

HOWARD HAMMERMAN

boldventurepress.com

This edition published
November 2017

© 2017 Howard Hammerman. All Rights Reserved.

ISBN-13: 978-1548926571
Retail cover price: $14.95 USA
Available in eBook edition

Printed and bound in the United States.

Acknowledgements

A part of me believes that only magic keeps airplanes from falling from the sky. The thrill of flying a small plane, feeling the wheels leaves the ground, has stayed with me more than 17 years since I last had the experience. For all those thrills, I would like to thank my flight instructors.

This book would not have been written without the contributions and support of my wife, Helen. Besides reading numerous drafts and suggesting a woman's point of view, she continually encouraged me to improve my craft. Her command of the English language contributed greatly to any literary quality the book may possess. Thank you my love.

Sarasota and Manatee counties have numerous writers-support and critique groups. I am fortunate to be part of several, including the Sarasota Fiction Writers' Association. This book owes its existence to the Florida Writer's Association Manatee critique group and its leader, Dona Lee Gould. Thank you, my friends.

Thanks also to Eric Wyatt, my first fiction teacher, who showed me the basics of the writing craft.

Finally, I want to thank friends and neighbors who have suffered through early drafts of this story during its five-year gestation. Thanks for both your encouragement and corrections.

Howard Hammerman
Sarasota, Florida
2017

Prolog

Here are some things you need to know about flying:

1. It is the forward motion of the airplane that keeps it in the air. The wings are flat on the bottom and curved on the top. The air takes longer to go over the top than the bottom and that, in turn, creates the partial vacuum called "lift." If a plane travels too slowly, it will have the aerodynamics of a rock.

2. The Second World War and then the Korea conflict produced a lot of pilots. Many people thought that a significant number of these men, once they returned home, would purchase personal airplanes for family vacations. They were wrong. There was a period of about two decades when virtually no single-engine airplanes were manufactured.

3. Cessna was a leading manufacturer of single-engine airplanes. The one that Dan owns in the story is a Cessna Cardinal. It is a four-place plane with two large doors and back seat. It sits low to the ground with the large wing above the cockpit. The interior has about as much room as a 1960 Volkswagen Beatle.

4. The Federal Aviation Administration (FAA) regulates all aspects of flying. Pilots must past recurring tests, and almost all airplanes must receive inspections at least once a year.

5. Flying is very expensive. Flying one's own airplane can be a wonderful experience. You get to pick your time and destination. You are an active participant in the methods of flight. When everything is going well, you feel like a god. Then there are the moments of terror.

Chapter 1

Richard

Monday, June 16
Gaithersburg Maryland

"Hey, mon, dat you airplane?"

"Yes, it is." I continued to secure my single-engine airplane to the tarmac. The taxi driver was parked nearby and was waiting for me. I chose to ignore him. I was not in the mood to make a new friend.

"Me name's Richard," the driver persisted "What you call yo'self?"

"Dan Goldberg. Just call me Dan." There was a time when I would introduce myself as Dr. Dan Goldberg. But I was no longer a college professor. My position had been eliminated during a round of state budget cuts. Rather than uproot my family to take another teaching job, I decided to become a self-employed consultant — one of the thousands plying their trades in and around our nation's capital.

"Okay, Daniel, we be friends, right?" He spoke in a musical way. Every third syllable was emphasized transforming my name into something more exotic. It reminded me of rum-filled nights the one time my wife, Beth, and I visited Jamaica.

I shook his hand, and we both smiled. His smile stretched from ear to ear, and it was impossible not to smile back even though my smile was a faint reflection of his broad grin. It seemed that we were at opposite ends of the emotional spectrum. Yet, it felt good to smile. It was my first smile in many days and, in this our first encounter, I was grateful to Richard for changing my mood.

We loaded my baggage into the taxi's trunk and headed for the Marriot. "Look at dat giant, white building mon. Dat a gold statue on top. Do you know what dat is?"

"Yes, it's the Mormon temple. Richard, I've lived and worked in the Washington area for more than a decade."

"Oh, okay, just so you know. I'll get you to the hotel real quick."

"That'll be great. I have a lot of work to do." To emphasize my point, I extracted a notepad from my computer case and pretended to work. But Richard didn't take the hint.

"Daniel, you married?"

"Yes."

"How long you been married?"

It was really none of his business, but I answered anyway. "Fourteen years." The year we were married I was a graduate student, and Beth was a newly minted third-grade teacher. We were happy then. No airplane, no children, no debts, no house, no lawn. We never fought about money because we had none.

"Ah, dat's good, mon. You got children?"

"Yes, I have two daughters. Amy's ten, Sarah's twelve."

"Dat's good too. A mon needs a family."

I wasn't sure I still had a family. At the end of our fight the night before, Beth said. "Can't you see that we can't afford your stupid aviation hobby? We're living on our credit cards and not putting anything away for the girls' college. You need to sell the airplane and get a job. Get rid of the plane, or I'm leaving! Or better yet, you're leaving! You can sleep in the hangar with your aluminum mistress."

In many ways, the airplane was my mistress. Most pilots learn their craft in the military. Even though I came of age during the Vietnam War, I avoided the draft and the military. Yet I always wanted to be a pilot. Once I started my own consulting business, I took the lessons and earned my wings. Then I needed an airplane.

I fell in love at first sight. We met at a rural airport in Virginia. Vines covered her landing gear. Her paint was chipped and faded. A bird had built its nest in her right wing.

I had to have her. "When did you last fly her?" I asked the broker.

"I've never flown the plane. I'm just showing it for the owner. I think he flew it about a year ago. That was before his heart attack. He died soon afterward, and his widow needs the cash. That's why it's for sale."

She was just the plane I wanted. She wasn't fast, but her large doors and high wings would make it easy for my wife to get in and fly with me. I gave the broker a deposit and prepared a sales pitch to my wife. "Think of all the money we'll save by flying ourselves rather than using the airlines. We can visit your parents more often. And when the girls go to college, we'll be able to fly to visit all the time."

Beth said "yes," and I bought the plane.

I housed her in her own hangar, cleaned her and bought her new electronics. We spent many Saturdays together just hanging out at the airport. I would polish her wings and side and show her off to the other pilots. She returned my love by flying straight and landing safely.

I tried to share my love with my family. Beth flew with me a few times but never felt comfortable in the air. Besides, threesomes never work.

Once I started paying off one credit card bill by taking a loan through another, Beth's attitude moved from indifference to hate.

I guess only rich men can afford to have mistresses. The previous night's fight made it clear to me — the plane will have to go.

Richard shouted a question over the divider as I started to draft a for sale ad in my mind. "Hey, Daniel how fast can it go?"

"How fast can what go?"

"Your airplane, how fast can it go?"

"Oh, it can fly about 110 miles per hour. Why?"

"If you had to go to Miami, Florida, how long would it take you?"

"A lot depends on the weather, but normally about two days."

Richard returned to his driving, and I returned to the depressing realization that my girlfriend and I would have to part ways. After a while, he asked, "How many kilos can you carry in dat airplane?"

I had heard about pilots getting asked to transport drugs. I decided to play along.

"I don't know about kilos, but I can carry about three hundred pounds," I said this with a smile. This will be a good story to tell my wife.

Richard punched numbers into a small calculator as he drove. Then he called someone using his cell phone. I lost interest and started to draft a "for sale" advertisement for my plane on a scrap of paper.

The driver ended his conversation at the same time that we pulled up to the front door of the hotel. I was ready to leave, but he stopped me. "Okay, mon here's the deal. You fly to a small airport near Miami. Me friend, he gives you two suitcases. You bring them back, and I give you $100,000."

My mouth dropped open. Was this the answer to my problems? I could tell my wife that I had a client in Florida. Two days down, two days back, and all our money problems would be solved. We would pay off our credit cards and get rid of the monthly payments on the plane. I could buy my wife the new car that she wanted and maybe even put some money away for my daughters' college funds.

But, of course, he wanted me to carry drugs. If I were caught, I'd go to jail.

"No, I can't do that," I said and started to open the back door.

The driver was ready for me. "Okay, mon," he countered without taking a breath, "I can see that you're a smart business-man. You deliver the suitcases, and I give you $200,000."

That got my attention. I could buy a new, faster plane. I wouldn't have to look for a job. I wouldn't have to sleep in the hangar. Maybe with a new plane, Beth would become more inter-ested in flying. The money would solve so many problems. I got my family into this financial mess, I had to get us out.

But what kind of a drug dealer solicits a mule minutes after he meets him? Richard could be an undercover cop assigned to entrap naive pilots. The image of Beth visiting me in jail had a sobering effect.

"How do I know that you'll pay me?"

"Look, we be businessmen. We pay you half before you leave and half when you get back. Just dis one time, mon."

"Can I think about it?"

"Sure ting, mon, you tink about it," Richard said releasing my arm. "How long you be here?"

"Four days. I'm teaching at the Parklawn Building in Rock-ville."

"Da Parklawn building! I know that building real good, mon. Don't worry! I be your driver all dis week. No charge for dis trip. How I reach you?"

His hand was out, and I gave him my business card, pausing only to write my cell phone number on the back. It was a reflex action, the result of years of soliciting business around the Washington Beltway.

Richard waved as he drove away. Only then did I realize that he had my home address and cell phone number while I had only his first name. As I pushed a cart loaded with my suitcase, computer, and a box of books, into the air-conditioned lobby, I started shivering, but not from the change in temperature. I had a plan.

Chapter 2

Change of Heart

I called my wife as soon as I got into my room. She picked up on the first ring. Her voice conveyed anger and concern. "Are you okay?"

"Yes, I'm fine. No problems with the flight. I'm at the hotel."

"Then you landed some time ago. Why didn't you call?"

"I'm sorry. I got to talking with the taxi driver and forgot. Is everything all right?"

"Dan, you promised to call when you landed."

There was a silence while I tried to find the words to apologize harder.

Beth continued. "I took Sara to the orthodontist to be fitted for braces. They needed a thousand-dollar deposit, and when I tried to put it on my MasterCard, it was declined. Didn't you pay that bill?"

"I paid the minimum, but we're carrying a large balance. I guess we're too close to the limit. Can we pay them next week?"

Beth sighed. "Yes, with all the business we give them, they trust us. When will you get your next check?"

"Friday. I'll get online and move some money around tonight." In the back of my mind, I visualized walking into the orthodontist's sleek office. I would dump a plastic bag full of hundred-dollar bills on the smug receptionist's desk and say, "Is that enough?" I smiled thinking about the look on her face.

"Dan, the car stalled when I was at a red light."

"Did it stall every time?"

"No, almost every time. Should I take it to the shop?"

"No, we can't handle another bill right now. When you need to stop, just put the car in neutral and keep your foot on the gas. Keep the RPMs over 2500. That should keep it from stalling."

"Yes, and I'll use more gas. We really need a new car, Dan. You know that my Dad has offered to buy us one. Think of it as a safety issue for the girls."

Beth's father was rich. He was a partner in a prestigious law firm in White Plains, New York. He showed his disdain for his son-in-law by writing checks. I hated him.

"Let's hold off for now. You know I don't like to be obligated to your father. Besides, I just got a great lead on a new project."

"I thought you just got to the hotel." Beth was quick, but I was quicker.

"I checked my email before I called you. I'll have more details tomorrow."

Beth didn't press for details. If she did, I would have told her about Richard's offer. She would have told me that I was crazy, and we would have laughed about it. But she didn't ask. We were both tired of fighting. Instead, we said that we loved each other in the mechanical way that married couples do and said good night.

***

It's important to maintain a routine while traveling on business. That afternoon I unpacked my suitcase and stored my clothes in the dresser and then arranged the desk the way I liked it with my laptop in the center. I checked for email messages and contacted previous clients to see if I could find new consulting assignments. That's the hardest part of being self-employed — When working, you don't have time to market your talents, and when you're marketing, you don't have time to work. That afternoon there were no new leads.

But I wasn't really interested in my consulting business. I was distracted. My mind was flying to Florida. Just for fun, I opened the navigation program on my computer and started planning the trip. A thousand miles at 110 miles per hour would require a bit more than nine hours of flying. That's too much for one day. I could stop overnight in South Carolina and visit my brother. I would do the same thing on the way back. My brother owned a successful restaurant and catering business.

My calculations filled two pages of scratch paper. In my mind, I was already spending the money. But was Richard's offer real? How could I trust him?

***

An hour later, I was sitting at the bar in the hotel's restaurant eating dinner when I heard someone ask, "Excuse me, can you please pass the ketchup?" Turning, I saw an attractive woman two stools away. I smiled and handed her the condiment. Our eyes locked and she smiled at me. "Is your book interesting?" she asked.

"Not very, I just hate to eat alone, so I always bring a book." The first thing I noticed was her long black hair and the silver clasp that held it back from her face. She was about 35, moderately fit. She had a slight bulge over the waistband of her gray skirt rather similar to the way extra pounds displayed themselves on my wife's torso. A jacket matching her skirt hung over the back of her chair and contrasted nicely with her short-sleeved white blouse.

Her jewelry consisted of an expensive looking watch on her left wrist and a set of silver bracelets on her right. She wore a small gold cross attached to a gold chain around her neck. I noted all this and concluded that she was traveling on business.

But most of all, during those first moments of our first meeting, I was captivated by the color of her skin. It had the color of cappuccino when the barista uses too much milk.

"I know what you mean. I also hate to eat alone," she said. "Can I join you?"

"That'll be great. Let's take a table."

Did those words come out of my mouth? Normally, I'm shy when meeting new people, especially women. But the conversation with Richard must have changed me. In my mind, I was a highly paid drug transporter. I felt a boldness I hadn't felt in a long time.

As luck would have it, there was an empty table nearby. I brought my hamburger, fries, and beer. She brought her salad, purse, and jacket. We sat across from each other. I sank into the depth of her eyes.

"My name's Maria Sanchez, what's yours?"

"Dan Goldberg." We exchanged business cards. Hers proclaimed that she was an account manager for Juarez Properties, Inc. based in New York City.

She asked me about my work, and I gave a slightly exaggerated version of the truth. In contrast to most people, Maria seemed interested in the statistics classes that I taught for the Federal government.

There was an awkward moment when we finished eating. I signed my check and got out of my chair. "It's been really nice meeting you. Maybe we'll meet again this week." I held out my hand for a business-like handshake.

She ignored it. "Let's have some wine in the lobby. My boss is buying. It's too early to go back to our rooms and watch TV." She had a cute mix of accents. Sometimes I could hear the streets of New York. Sometimes there was a hint of the Caribbean. Two glasses of Chardonnay appeared, and we found an unused couch.

I told her that I was a pilot and owned my own airplane. It's possible that I exaggerated about the size and speed of my plane.

"That's so exciting," she said, "Tell me about flying."

I described my more interesting flying adventures but stopped when her gaze began to wander. I searched for a way to redirect the conversation and said, "You sound like you're from New York."

She giggled. "Actually, I'm from Puerto Rico. My family moved to New York City when I was thirteen."

"What does Juarez Properties do?"

"We're a national and international real estate firm. When I started, I was an agent. I worked with Latino families in New York who wanted to buy real estate in Florida. Now I mostly work with wealthy buyers from Latin America. I show high-end properties and translate between the buyers and sellers. That's why I'm in Washington this week. I was supposed to work with a client from Honduras, but he had visa problems and was delayed."

At the time, that sounded reasonable. I pictured Maria walking into a condo and explaining the features, in Spanish, to an older, overweight couple while the selling agent looked on and smiled.

In fact, I didn't care how she earned a living. My gaze dropped from her face to her chest. I saw just a bit of white lace peeking through her partly unbuttoned blouse. The cross rested directly above the lace reminding me that everything below was forbidden territory.

We finished the wine and walked to the elevator together. We said, "good night" when she got off on the second floor. I continued on to the third. After she had left, I could still hear the lilt of her accent and see the way her teeth showed when she smiled.

Then Richard called.

"Hello, Daniel Did you enjoy your supper?"

"Oh hi, Richard, I'm glad you called. I'm still thinking about your offer."

"Relax, Mon, no problem. Look, Daniel, what time you need to be at your work tomorrow? I come pick you up."

"I need to be there at 8:30. You need to pick me up at 7:30."

"No problem. I be dere in plenty of time. And, mon, when you done work, I need a favor. There's a man in New Jersey dat owe me money. I want you to fly me there and bring me back. And I pay you mon, how about dat? The taxi driver, *he* pay for a ride!"

Richard was delighted with his joke and laughed. I didn't. "Where in New Jersey do you need to go?"

"It be near Atlantic City. Me friend, he owes me money, and I give you half."

I wanted more details, but Richard was done. "We talk together in the morning, mon."

Later that night, when I got into bed, I was still thinking about Maria. I went through the whole evening in my mind and remembered she was eating a salad. Why would a person eating a salad ask for ketchup? My God, was she flirting with me? That had never happened before.

In my dream, I began to see Maria again — not all of her, just parts of her. I remembered her light brown skin. I remembered the hem of her skirt where it lay just above her knee. My mind followed the curve of her thigh from the hem of her skirt to her waist. In my half-sleep, my hand traveled that path and imagined pulling up her skirt. She responded by closing her eyes and catching her breath. Then her skirt evaporated, and I found she was wearing my wife's white cotton panties. I was hoping for something black and silky.

In that weird space between waking and sleeping, I created a second draft featuring black satin lingerie. Happy with my edit, my dream hand continued to explore Maria's body while my real hand traveled to my crotch. The rest of her clothes melted away and my imagination manufactured a composite woman made of Maria's hair, face, and legs and Beth's familiar crotch, breasts, and neck.

Like a demented child playing with plastic toys, I combined and re-combined the body parts. In my fantasy, the Maria-Beth creature was on top of me. Her breasts and her hair dangled in my face. As we moved, her hair whipped my face. I surrendered to the fantasy and could almost feel her breasts on my chest. The crescendo grew and grew and finally climaxed dropping me into a deep and dreamless sleep.

Chapter 3

Bad news

I found Richard in the lobby the next morning chatting with the restaurant's receptionist.

"Hello, Daniel," he said with a smile as bright as the morning sun. I began to like this guy with his ever-optimistic outlook. "Let me introduce you to my friend, Cora. Cora, dis here be *Doctor* Daniel Goldberg da world's leading expert at sumptin he teaches at da Parklawn building." Cora and I awkwardly shook hands. We both knew that Richard was full of it, but neither of us wanted to leave the jovial cloud he carried with him. Cora led us to a table, and I signaled for coffee.

I was just finishing my second cup when Maria came in. She smiled at me, and immediately I forgot where I was and began a re-run of last night's dream. Then Richard broke the spell.

"Hey, mon, you all right?" He followed my gaze and smiled. "She's pretty, but take me advice Daniel. She be trouble! Remember your family."

An Hispanic-looking man, dressed in a suit joined her, and I felt a jolt of crazy jealousy. I concealed it by gobbling my eggs.

After breakfast, Richard helped me retrieve the boxes of textbooks from my room. When he saw my rumpled bed, he said, "Daniel, you dog! You and your big bamboo had a time wit that lovely lady downstairs. My, my you do not move slow mon! But don't you worry, your secret be safe wit me".

Just what I needed right now — a witness to an affair I didn't have. I never had an affair. I had enough trouble keeping one woman happy, let alone two.

"I slept alone last night she wasn't here."

"Ok, mon. Have it your way," he said laughing.

Richard and I were just a bit out of sync. He was living in a hopeful future while I was I was stuck regretting the past.

Richard put my stuff in the trunk of the yellow taxi and, with a flourish; he invited me to join him in the front seat signaling a change in our relationship. "Richard," I said, "I'm happy to take you to New Jersey this evening, but I need to know exactly where we're going. And I'll have to charge you eight hundred dollars for the round trip. Do you still want to go?"

Richard laughed as the taxi found the entrance to the Beltway. "Hey, Daniel, don't worry. Here, look at dis."

He handed me an envelope containing ten one-hundred-dollar bills. Scrawled on the outside were the words, "Berlin, New Jersey." Berlin was a small town about ten miles North of Atlantic City. It had a well-maintained public airport for private planes. The runway was long, wide and flat.

"There's a thousand dollars here. I only need eight hundred."

"Don't worry, Daniel. It's okay. The man I need to meet, he owes me two thousand and, as I say on the phone, I give you half."

It was a little after nine by the time Richard, the boxes, and I made it through security and up to the computer-equipped class-room on the sixth floor. Bertha Roberts, the training officer, was pacing the hall, obviously annoyed. A heavyset woman in her mid-fifties, Bertha normally wore her glasses on a silver chain around her neck. That morning the glasses swung back and forth like a metronome.

"Dan, where've you been? The class should be starting now." Looking over her shoulder, I saw some of the students sitting at their desks. One of the students, an attractive African-American woman, was even studying a copy of my textbook. That was unusual. Most of the government employees who took my class had little interest in statistics and were there only because their supervisors forced them to attend.

"I'm so sorry, Bertha," I said, "Traffic was terrible." In answer to her silent question, I continued: "This is Richard, my taxi driver."

Richard focused his thousand-watt smile over the boxes in his hands. "Dat is right, Misses. Da traffic, it be horrible on da Beltway. But how you get to look so pretty so early in the morning?"

Bertha blushed and waved him away. Turning to me, she said, "Dan, we need to talk. Please stop by my office at lunchtime, okay?"

Richard put the boxes on my desk and said, "Don't forget mon, I pick you up at 4 pm. Den we go to New Jersey." Then he left taking my happy feelings with him.

As I unpacked my laptop, the African-American woman came to my desk. "Hi, I'm Michelle; I just joined the staff of the training department. Do you mind if I sit in on your class?"

"Not at all I'm happy to have you."

The morning went well, and we stopped for lunch at 11:30. It felt good to be back in the classroom. I missed teaching.

I went to the basement and used my bank's ATM to increase the Goldberg family's net worth by five hundred dollars. I bought a sandwich from the "grab and go" line and went back to my desk. I had just taken the third bite when Bertha came in. "Dan, are you done with your lunch?" It wasn't really a question.

"Sure," I responded. I threw most of my lunch in the trash. Something in Bertha's made me wonder if my career would follow the same arc.

I had been in Bertha's small, crowded office before. Most of her wall space was filled to overflowing with training manuals. A large whiteboard held the place of honor near her desk showing classes scheduled for the next three months. My class was listed among them. But something wasn't right. My current class dates were written in red while the remaining class dates were black.

At the start of our last meeting, Bertha pushed the mountain of file folders aside to create a clear space for us to work together. We became friends and, during breaks, we shared stories about our children. Today the file folders remained untouched. She was all business.

"Look, Bertha, if this is about my getting here late, I apologize. This is the first time it's happened in two and a half years, and it won't happen again. We covered all the material we normally cover. The class is going well."

"No Dan, it's not about you getting here late. You're doing a great job. Your evaluations are excellent." She paused. I knew there was a "but" coming.

"You're probably not aware of it, but we've been under pressure to reduce the number of outside contractors and bring the training in-house."

"I've heard rumors, but I didn't think it applied to my classes."

Bertha turned away from me and looked out the window. I followed her gaze and saw only the neighboring parking structure and the hazy sky.

"It didn't apply, at least until recently. We've not been able to do so with your class because of the highly technical nature of your subject material." She paused and looked for a file on her desk. She found the one we wanted and handed me three neatly-typed pages secured with a staple. I glanced at the top of the first page. It was Michelle's resume.

"Dan, as you know we've been able to hire Michelle. As you can see, she also has a Ph.D. She's taught a course similar to yours when she worked at the community college." Bertha pulled a tissue box from her bottom drawer and blew her nose.

"Bertha," I began, "I'm sure Michelle is an excellent resource. I'm sure we can work together."

She ignored my remark. "Dan, after this week, Michelle will teach your class. I'm sorry, but the rest of your contract is canceled. Here's your formal notice. I was able to get accounting to cut your final check. It's in the envelope as well."

I tried to find the words to respond to Bertha. The monthly check more than covered our mortgage payment. Without it, we would have to rely on my other contracts. The problem was, I had no other contracts. Beth and I would never be able to make ends meet even without the airplane expenses.

The silence hung heavily in the room. A cold sweat broke out on my forehead. How would I explain this to Beth? I tried to find the words to further argue my case but realized it would be pointless. The decision had already been made a bureaucratic level much higher than Bertha's.

Bertha sat in her chair waiting for me to leave. I wanted to get angry at her, but I couldn't. Finally, she broke the silence saying, "Dan, you better get going. Your class is starting soon."

Michelle was waiting for me in the classroom. Somehow she knew about the meeting. She started to come up to my desk to offer sympathy, but I just looked at her and shook my head. I didn't want her sympathy. I wanted her job.

Chapter 4

Cocaine in the afternoon

The rest of the class went by in a blur. I'd taught the class dozens of times, and I wrote the textbook. On autopilot, I told the same jokes I had told before and got the same groans and titters.

We completed the material I wanted to cover by 3:30. I mechanically asked for questions and was grateful for the students' indifference. No hands came up.

Michelle stayed after the others left. She came to my desk with the same sorrowful look she had since lunch. "Listen, Dan, I had nothing to do with this."

"I know that. That's the way it works in contracting. Don't worry about me, I have lots of other contracts," I lied.

She knew I was lying, and her face became even more sorrowful. "Well best of luck, Dan. Do you mind if I sit in on the rest of the class?"

I didn't care. I had my check. *Maybe I should just blow off the rest of the class and go home,* I thought. "Sure, no problem. In fact, why don't you teach the segment tomorrow morning and I'll give feedback." *That's great,* I thought with a mental scowl, *I can teach you to take over my job.*

"Great, I'd really like that," she said sincerely.

Once she left, I went to the ATM in the basement to deposit the government check and half of cash Richard gave me. Then I transferred $500 into Beth's credit card account. I checked my email but didn't find any new prospects for work.

I found Richard waiting at the curb wearing his familiar big smile. "Hey, mon, where you been? I be waiting. They make me move two times, but I come back."

He led me to an old black Cadillac two-door sedan. It once had a landau top, but most of the covering had worn away with at least twenty-five years of sun and weather. The back wheel sported an original hubcap, but the front wheel was bare. Duct tape strained to hold the headlight in place.

"What happened to your taxi?" I asked as he put my laptop in the back seat next to a black, nylon duffle bag.

"Da taxi? She be in da shop. This be me personal car."

I sat in the front as Richard turned into the afternoon traffic. "What da matter mon? You look like you lost you puppy."

"They told me that my contract was over. This is my last week teaching."

"It doesn't matter Daniel. Da money it comes, da money it goes. What be important is you take care of your family. Dere always be a way to make more money."

I ignored Richard and entered Beth's number on my cell phone. I had to tell her the bad news, and I was dreading the task. I almost pressed the call button when I noticed that we were on the way to the airport, not my hotel. *Oh, my God*, I thought, *I promised to take Richard to New Jersey tonight!* I had completely forgotten about it.

I needed to get back to the hotel. I was torn between a desire to drink myself into a stupor or start making marketing calls. I needed to make more money, and at the same time, I was sick and tired of trying to do it.

Maybe I'm just not good at this consulting business. Maybe I should polish my resume and start looking for a real job. Maybe I can get a job with the government like Michelle did. Or maybe

I should contact the community college where she was teaching.
Now that she's with the feds, there must be a vacancy. Screw the
airplane. I'm not flying anywhere tonight.

"Richard, no, I'm not flying anywhere tonight. I'm not in the
mood. I'm tired and worried, and all I want is a beer and a bed —
maybe more than one beer." The thought of teaching the next
three days on a lame duck contract turned my stomach. Richard
didn't reply.

I extracted the remaining hundred dollars bills from my wallet.
"Here is part of your money. I'll write you a check for the rest as
well as for the cab rides when we get back to the hotel." Richard
said nothing and didn't even acknowledge my declaration with a
nod. He made no move to collect cash. The little pile sat on the
dashboard, a mediator to our dispute. Silently, he maneuvered the
car into the left-hand lane. I assumed he would turn left at the
light and take me back to the hotel.

We were in the front of the line, waiting for the light to change
when he finally spoke. "So Daniel, you say you want to go to
your hotel and drink da beer. But Daniel, me friend, dis not be a
taxi, dis be *me* car, and I take me car where I want to go. And now
we go to you plane."

I was scared and angry.

Who the fuck does he think he is?

I realized how little I knew about Richard. I was beginning
to realize how his "no problem" charms had clouded my usual
good judgment. I thought about dashing out, braving the four
lanes of traffic to get away. Instead, I cleared Beth's number from
my cell phone and started dialing 911.

Just then the light turned green. Richard floored the accelera-
tor, making an illegal U-turn in the middle Wisconsin Avenue
during rush hour. The force of the turn pushed me off balance
and, as I tried to recover, he grabbed the cell phone from my hand.
He ignored the chorus of outraged car horns then cut in front of

a delivery truck with inches to spare as he swerved into the parking lot of a large shopping mall.

"Where're you going? Stop the car!" I demanded.

He ignored me and sped behind the stores and into a service alley. I shouted to a group of workers relaxing with their cigarettes on a loading dock. They didn't hear me.

There was a high block wall on the right and the back doors of stores on the left. We started in the bright June sunlight. Each steel door had the occupant's name in stenciled letters. After the tenth door, the alley was in deep shadow.

The alley made a sharp left turn. I hoped it would empty into the parking lot at the opposite end of the mall so I could make my escape. But there was no exit. We passed a few more stores and came to a dead end. As he slowed, Richard directed the car against the right-hand wall making it impossible for me to get out.

Then he turned off the engine. Until that moment, I hadn't taken the jovial Jamaican very seriously. Now I was trapped in his car, down a blind alley, without my cell phone.

Richard turned to me, "So you be tired and discouraged mon. I know what you feel. When I lived in Jamaica, me father and me picked bananas and pineapples for Dole fruit. When da fruit be ripe, we go to the fields, and we pick all day an all night. Sometimes we work sixteen hours straight in da fields wit the bugs and da snakes. Da boss he weigh the baskets, and we be paid by the pound, and sometimes he cheats on the scales. Do you tink we get discouraged Mon? We be discouraged, but we keep working because we have to — for da family. But we did get tired sometimes. And for dis we hab a solution."

Richard stopped talking and pulled out a knife. It was long and skinny. When he pressed a button, a thin blade popped out and glistened in the alley's half-light. I moved as far away as I could and grabbed my computer case to use as a shield.

Was he going to kill me?

"Not to worry, me friend. I won't kill you, not today," he said with a chuckle. Then he removed a small mirror and a glassine envelope of powder from his fanny pack. He used the blade to move a small portion of the powder onto the mirror and then arranged the powder into two rows. "Dis here be cocaine. It will clear your mind, mon."

My fear gradually morphed into curiosity. My only experience with illegal drugs was the time when Beth and I went to Jamaica for our honeymoon. We enjoyed the island "vibe" that included the rum cocktails, reggae music, roast goat and the omnipresent smell of marijuana. On our first night there, I gave our waiter a ten-dollar bill and asked if he could get us some "ganja." A few hours later he came to our room with a shopping bag full of the stuff.

That bag kept us very high and happy for the rest of the week. Sara, our older daughter, arrived precisely nine months after our trip. Soon after that, the pressures of family and career got in the way of that kind of reckless behavior.

Richard rolled one of my hundred-dollar bills into a tube. He focused the tube on the left-hand line and inhaled. When he finished, he shook his body like a dog coming out of a lake.

"Now you. Just inhale like you be smelling a flower." I spent about two seconds making my decision. At first, I wasn't going to do it. Then I reconsidered.

What the hell? Richard was forcing me to do something I always wanted to do. I inhaled.

The effect was amazing. The confusion, depression, and tiredness disappeared. I closed my eyes for a few seconds. When I opened them, Richard was smiling. "You feel better mon?" he asked.

"Yes."

The analytical part of my mind knew that once we were at

the airport, there would be a thousand ways I could escape my captor. But now I didn't care. Was it the cocaine or my enthusiasm for the adventure?

Fuck the credit cards, fuck Brenda and her budget. I'm doing this!

As Richard backed out of the alley, the right side of the car scraped the wall removing a good deal of the paint and the Cadillac's passenger side mirror. Richard didn't seem to notice or care.

My nose had turned numb. Then I remembered my wife. I wanted her to know how good it felt.

Maybe Beth and I should try cocaine. What would it feel like to have sex while high on cocaine?

"Let me have my cell phone," I demanded, "I need to call my wife."

She didn't answer, and I had to leave a message. "Hi, Beth it's me. Class went well. I'm going out to dinner with a new business associate, so I'll have to turn off my phone. I'll talk to you in the morning. Hope all is well."

I pressed the end button. "Very good, mon," Richard shouted as we turned onto the highway. "We fly."

Chapter 5

Airborne

"You must always follow a written checklist," my flight instructor said the first time that we got into an airplane. He repeated it again and again until it became a mantra that I scrupulously followed while I was learning to fly. After earning my wings, I continued to follow his instructions each and every time I flew. But the cocaine flowing through my veins convinced me the checklist was unimportant. There was no need to check a sample of fuel for contaminants because my enhanced sense of smell told me the fuel was just fine. It wasn't necessary to check each of the navigation lights, I simply put my hands on a wing and my old friends the red, green, and white light bulbs told me they were ready to illuminate as soon as I flipped the switch.

Ignoring the checklist was foolhardy. Flying under the influence was illegal. A small part of my brain knew this, but that part was aggressively suppressed by the rest of my psyche.

With Richard and his black duffle safely on board, I pressed the radio button and asked for weather and radio checks. The sole employee on duty that afternoon, replied, "We read you loud and clear, Mr. Goldberg. The wind is from the west at five miles an hour. There's a cold front coming that will probably bring a thunderstorm, but it won't be here until ten or eleven. Will you be returning to the airport later?"

"Yes, this is just a local flight."

"Okay, have a nice flight."

I taxied to the end of the runway and obtained clearance to fly the narrow corridor between Washington and Baltimore on my way east to New Jersey. I brought the engine up to full power, released the brakes, keeping the nose pointed at the runway's center line. The irony wasn't lost on Richard, who said, "Hey mon, we're doing another line." We were airborne before I could think of a snappy retort.

Flying the corridor requires concentration because of the three large airports, many small ones, and the numerous "no-fly" zones such as the White House and Capitol. Normally it is a white-knuckle experience. That Tuesday with my drug-enhanced awareness, I felt relaxed, confident, even arrogant. All the important landmarks stood out against the urban landscape as if some giant hand had inserted labels next to them. I was able to see the other planes before Air Traffic Control (ATC) advised me of their presence. I was certain that I was heading in the right direction at the best altitude. I was in the zone, flying intuitively.

Richard said nothing. We had reversed roles. Now I was in control. "Do you have any questions?" I asked as an American Airlines jet, crammed with several hundred souls, passed over our heads with a thousand feet to spare. Before he could respond, we were buffeted by the jet's wake. The plane rocked forward and back. The view through the windshield changed from land to sky. It only lasted a few seconds. I was ready for it and just held the controls steady. Richard wasn't. I watched with a perverse joy as Richard's smile disappeared and was replaced by a grimace of terror.

After the turbulence passed and he had enough breath to talk, he pointed to the aviation chart in my lap and asked, "What's that?"

"It's a special map that pilots use. It shows all the airports, restricted areas, cell phone towers, and major landmarks."

"Do it show *all* the airports? What about the private airports on people's land?"

"Yes, it shows those too."

Richard entered a number into his cell phone. He spoke for a while then asked, "Daniel, you know about latlon numbers?" He had to repeat this twice until I understood that he meant latitude and longitude.

"Yes, of course, what about them?" *Was he trying to teach me geography?*

Richard wrote two numbers and the word "Waterford" in the white space on the edge of my chart.

"I need you to take me to dis airport. It be a private field, no problem. You just drop me off dere."

I put the plane on autopilot and found the town of Waterford, New Jersey. Sure enough, there was the indication of a private airfield with a grass runway. I hated grass runways. They often had bumps and ruts that could damage my precious plane. I heard stories of pilots hitting deer while landing, with disastrous results to all parties.

"I don't know, Richard," I said. "Why don't I take you to Berlin as we agreed? It has a nice, long, paved runway. Landing on grass can damage my plane."

Without missing a beat, Richard reached into his pouch and pulled out ten more hundred dollar bills. "Daniel, me plans be changed," he demanded while waving the bills at me.

The extra thousand would make a welcome dent in my family's debts. But I sensed a note of urgency in Richard's voice and remembered my terror behind the shopping mall. "Fuck you, Richard. I don't care how much money you have in there. Let's just forget about this trip. I'm turning back to Gaithersburg." I rocked my wings slightly as if I was getting ready to make a U-turn.

"No, don't do it!" Richard shouted. "Here be another thousand.

I need to be at dat airport. It's getting late."

The extra money would bring the trip's total to three thousand dollars, about the same amount of my last government check. "Ok," I said, proud that I was able to get the better of the Jamaican. "I'll try to land there. But if I can't, we're going to Berlin."

That was a lie. I knew we were going to land at Waterford no matter what. At that moment, I felt I could do anything. The engine pulling us through the air was tuned to my heartbeat. The vibrations under my seat were linked to my nervous system. I could feel my fingers extending through the yoke, into the wings all the way to the ailerons where the wind flowing over my aluminum skin held the plane aloft. The airplane and I were a single living entity flying at 5500 feet. I never felt anything like this before. If we were not in controlled airspace, I would have tried to do a flip.

We passed out of the Baltimore controlled airspace and continued eastward into New Jersey. Soon we were over the Pine Barrens and out of flight controllers' domains. We were flying over acres of trees only occasionally interrupted by a road. In the distance, we could see the late afternoon sunlight reflecting off of the Atlantic City casino towers. Otherwise, the landscape was unmarred by human habitation.

The distance to the airport as displayed on the GPS's small screen steadily declined. When it was down to single digits, we spotted a large rectangle cut out of the trees and framed by a dirt road at one end, and steel electric transmission towers at the other. I reduced altitude to 1200 feet and flew over the towers shuddering to think what would happen if we caught a wheel in one of the cables.

Richard, the ever-helpful co-pilot, contributed, "Hey mon, you need to watch out for dem cables. Dey looks real close."

"Don't worry. We're at least 400 feet higher. Can you see your friend? Are you sure this is the right place?"

Richard made the call as I crossed the middle of the runway. "Henry, you dere?" After a pause, "Henry say he seeing your plane. He says the runway is all right, nice and smooth. He on it now."

Just then, I saw a man waving his arms. I turned left and flew parallel to the runway. I could see a tractor with its mowing attachment parked at one end. I continued two miles past the field and then turned left twice reducing power after each turn. We were on final approach and ready to land. I stayed at 1000 feet, and as soon as the power lines were behind us, I cut the engine back to idle. We needed to lose altitude quickly. I turned my ailerons sharply to the left while depressing the right rudder pedal to the floor. The maneuver destroyed the plane's lift, and we dropped like a stone.

"Who-ee," said Richard straining against the shoulder straps, "Watch out! We're going to crash!"

Just a taste of what you put me through. We hit the ground with the nose wheel in the middle of the runway and bounced back into the air. The end of the runway was just ahead, and I realized that I wouldn't be able to stop in time, so I added full power and brought the nose up intending to go around and try again. Too high. The stall-warning horn sounded, a blaring high-pitched monotone, and we began to fall despite the roaring engine.

I lowered the nose. The horn stopped but the trees were coming fast, so I raised the flaps. The reduced drag created additional speed, which, in turn, translated into the additional lift. Several trees to the right weren't as high as the others, so I turned to the gap and climbed out of the hole in the forest.

My passenger sat very straight and still. "Hey mon, you know how to fly dis ting?" he said in a soft voice.

"Yo, my man, you turn. You go land dere." Then I let go of the yoke. The plane veered to the right and started to fall.

Richard recoiled from the yoke as if it were a snake. "Holy shit mon, I'm sorry. You fly just fine."

I kept my hands on my lap as the plane started a lazy death spiral. Richard grabbed the yoke and pulled it to his chest which made the plane stall and triggered the horn again. I waited until I could see the sweat beading his forehead. Then he started to scream. "Daniel, please. We going to crash!"

We were 50 feet over the trees when I finally grabbed the yoke. We continued to circle, but this time, we were going up, not down. I wasn't done with my flying companion. "Richard, are you sure you wouldn't like to land?"

"No mon, you just fly it da way you do. I'll jus' sit."

Grinning maniacally, I maneuvered the plane past the field to line up for a second try. This time, we cleared the power lines by less than 100 feet. I could see a man, presumably Henry, sitting on a small motorcycle at the beginning of the runway.

Full flaps down, I cut the power, crossed the controls, and brought us down to 50 feet above the grass. But the plane was flying sideways. If the wheels touched the ground, we would crash. At the last possible moment, I uncrossed the controls and got the nose pointed in the right direction.

Seconds before the wheels touched the ground, a flock of pheasants flew directly in front of us. The wildfowl and my propeller merged. A puree of blood and feathers covered most of my windshield.

"Watch out, Daniel, more coming!"

I couldn't see them. Pieces of dead fowl obliterated my forward vision. We heard three thumps as three more cousins joined the avian suicide pact. There was nothing I could do about it. I didn't panic. If we stayed in the center of the runway, we'd be able to stop before hitting the trees.

Then I heard a crunching sound and the plane veered sharply to the left. A glance out my left-side window showed blood and feathers surrounding the left wheel cowling. The left wheel's brake mechanism was jammed. I pressed down on the right brake pedal to compensate, but the tires just skidded to the left on the grass.

I still didn't panic. *Once we leave the mowed portion, the high grass will stop us.*

"Christ Daniel, can't you stop dis ting?" Richard yelled.

I wasn't going to answer him. I had just realized that we weren't heading towards the benevolent high grass. We were skidding directly towards the parked tractor. That's when I panicked. If we crashed into the tractor, the plane would never fly again.

"Tighten your seat belt," I yelled as the right wing got closer and closer.

Finally, it was one of the runway ruts that saved us. My right wheel sank up to its axle. It became a pivot, swerving us away from destruction. We came to an ignoble stop with the left wing fifteen feet away from the tractor.

I could tell by his ashen face that Richard had forgotten to breathe. He was clasping his duffle bag to his chest like a life preserver.

Exhausted, I could feel pools of sweat on my back and in my armpits. When I turned off the engine, the quiet overwhelmed me. It was interrupted only by the chirps of the remaining pheasants.

"Dey singing for dey dead folks," Richard observed.

"I think its applause for my great flying."

"Ya mon, you good. You real good."

If only my flight instructor could see me now.

Chapter 6

Plans Change

Even before I opened the door, I knew we were in trouble. The mess on the windshield looked like I'd flown through a butcher shop, but that didn't bother me. Some water and a little elbow grease would clean it up. The real problem was the left wheel. I knew it was jammed. If it was bent, or if I blew the tire, we would be stuck.

The cowling over the wheel was a mess. It was dented and almost torn off its frame.

"God damn it, Richard," I yelled, "look what happened!"

Richard didn't respond to my harangue. It seemed to take all his resources to get his feet to the ground. His face was ashen — a new look for the jolly Jamaican. His distress was my only solace for the damage.

The motorcycle rider approached. He was young and like Richard, a Jamaican. Like his mentor, he wore his hair was in dreadlocks. "Richard," he said, "I thought for sure you were going to crash!"

What about me, asshole. Did you think Richard was flying the plane?

They embraced, and Richard said, "Henry, you must meet me good friend and first class pilot, Daniel. Daniel, dis be me friend and partner Henry."

I nodded in Henry's general direction. I didn't come to this

God-forsaken pheasant sanctuary to make new acquaintances. While they talked, I removed the wheel cowling. It was damaged beyond repair. Thankfully, aside from being clogged with bird parts and grass, the brakes and tire were okay. I removed the mess transferring some of the blood and mud to my clothes.

The three of us pushed the plane near the hangar, where I used a hose to wash the windshield. The two co-conspirators moved their business conference around the corner and out of earshot. As I worked, the breeze freshened. There was still plenty of sunlight since it was almost the longest day of the year. I was hot, hungry, and dirty — anxious to get back.

"Okay, Richard, can we leave now?" I asked when the two returned. I assumed that Henry was the person that owed Richard money.

"No, Daniel, Henry and me, we need to go see a man about da money. You fly by yourself to Atlantic City, and we meet you dere." I was getting more and more annoyed.

"What do you mean? Isn't Henry the man who owes you the money?"

Once again our roles reversed. I was now the student, and Professor Richard was teaching his course *Introduction to Drug Dealing 101.* "You see, Daniel, Henry he handles me business in New Jersey. We need to see a certain man together. We need to go right now."

Atlantic City International was less than thirty miles away. I could get there easily, but another takeoff and landing weren't part of the deal.

"How long will you be? It'll get dark soon, and there is a storm due to arrive in a few hours.

"Don't worry, we be there by ten o'clock. I call you when we're on our way."

I didn't like it. If we left Atlantic City at ten, I wouldn't get back to my hotel until after midnight.

"Richard, why don't you get back with Henry? I'll just fly back alone."

Although we had only known each other for a handful of hours, Richard had taken an advanced course in Dan Goldberg management and motivation. He pulled out his familiar roll of hundreds and peeled off twenty. "Here, Daniel. This be for da extra work. It be enough?"

"No, it's not enough. I need to replace the cowling."

Richard nodded and added ten more bills. "Is that enough?" he asked.

It was indeed enough. I now had six thousand dollars more than I had when I finished teaching that afternoon. Then Richard handed me a glassine envelope. "Here mon, this be a present for you. Use it when you get tired."

My patron extended his hand. We were businessmen. We had just completed a deal.

"You fly safely, Daniel." We were standing in shadows cast by the hanger. His dark skin merged with the shadows while his white smile floated in the darkness. It reminded me of the Cheshire Cat in the *Alice in Wonderland* story, and I shuddered.

Henry kicked the motorcycle to life. Richard climbed onto the back with his signature black bag over his shoulder. He waved once, and they vanished into the trees.

"It's okay," I told the surviving pheasants, "I'm doing this for my family."

But that was a rationalization. I had fallen down the rabbit hole as surely as Alice had done. Or was I more like Dorothy in *Wizard of Oz*? Both characters were trying to get home, yet with each passing hour, I was moving further and further from my goal.

With the cocaine out of my system, I had enough sense to perform a complete checklist before starting the engine. I had less fuel and no passenger, so the plane lifted into the air a comfortable distance from the end of the runway. I spiraled once to gain altitude and then headed northeast.

I didn't need the GPS to find the airport. The Atlantic City Expressway is a brightly-lit, four-lane concrete ribbon that bisects Southern New Jersey's dense forest and shrubs. I headed north until I found the expressway, and then followed it east to the airport. The tower welcomed me as soon as I called and directed me to one of their miles-long, perfectly level, concrete runways. When I taxied to the fuel depot, a young man waved me to a parking spot and said, "Welcome to Atlantic City, sir. Are you staying the night? Do you want me to fill your tanks?"

"No, I'm staying just a few hours. I don't need fuel. Where can I get some food?"

"The restaurants are in the main terminal, on the other side of the airport. Normally, one of us would drive you there and bring you back, but I'm the only one working now. In fact, I'm leaving in a few minutes. We have vending machines, a micro-wave, and coffee inside. Of course, you can walk, but it would take at least a half hour each way."

I wanted to be ready when Richard called, so I settled for vending-machine microwave pizza. Then I made myself comfort-able in the pilot's lounge.

I was mad about the damage to my plane and tried to blame Richard, but really, I was mad at myself. If I hadn't bought the plane, my family we wouldn't be in a financial mess. If I hadn't agreed to fly to New Jersey, I wouldn't be sitting here waiting. That was just the highlights of a long chain of "ifs."

That's enough. If Richard doesn't call before ten, I'll fly back alone.

At nine-thirty, the fuel jockey joined me. "I'm leaving now. We leave the pilot's lounge open all night, but you better tie down your plane. The wind is picking up, and the weather service says we'll get rain."

He was right. I found my plane rocking back and forth on its landing gear. I always carried ropes in the small luggage compartment behind the second seat of the plane just for that purpose. It was accessible from both the interior and from a small exterior door. I used the space as a catch-all for spare parts, tools, and ropes.

Something was holding the ropes down. Did something break during that damn landing? Using my flashlight, I found the problem. Richard's black duffle bag was lying on top of the ropes. What the hell was it doing there? I saw him drive away with a black bag over his shoulder. Did he switch bags? Why?

I pulled out the bag and opened the zipper. It was filled with cash. The bills were gathered in bundles, each secured by a rubber band. It had to be drug money, and I had unknowingly become a drug-money transporter. Richard left me literally holding the bag.

I laughed. Here I was taking all these risks for a few thousand dollars when, in the back of my plane, was a bag with a king's ransom. I took one bundle and stuffed it into my pants.

Just then a gust of wind caught my left wing and tried to lift the plane off the ground. I returned to the task at hand. I secured the plane and went inside with my new-found treasure.

The pilot's lounge was empty and quiet. I tried calling Richard's phone, then Henry's, but got no answer. I could hear my wife's voice in my head. *Leave! Come home! Dump the money in the garbage!*

Instead, I went into the men's room, locked the door and counted my confiscated bundle. When I was done, I had arranged ten stacks of bills, each stack ten high, on the shelf to the left of the sink. One hundred bills, each bill worth one hundred dollars. I had ten thousand dollars in front of me, and there were many, many more bundles in the back of my plane. Did Richard even know how many bundles were in his duffle? Would he miss one?

I resolved to keep the money. If I was an accomplice, I was going to be paid like one. I separated the bills into four stacks and put them in the pockets of my computer case.

Richard's call came a few minutes after ten. "OK, Daniel, you ready to fly?" He was out of breath.

"Richard, where are you? Are you here at the airport? I'm at the fuel depot. Ask someone to let you through the gate. We have to leave soon. The weather's changing, and they're predicting rain." I wasn't going to confront him about the money until we were together.

"Look, mon. We had to move. We not too far away. Look on your map. We be west of Ocean City in New Jersey."

"You want me to pick you up in Ocean City?" Ocean City, a small seaside town just south of Atlantic City, has a small, adequate, airport with one paved runway.

"No, Daniel, please listen. You must fly to Ocean City den go west. Henry, he got da numbers, but you must hurry mon."

Henry got on the phone. "Here be the numbers. They will take you to a housing development what got no houses. Der just be roads but no houses. We hab two cars and we'll park one at each end of the street. You just land between the cars."

"Just land between the cars? What the hell are you talking about? You want me to land on a city street?" To say it was illegal was a gross understatement. It would be dangerous during the daytime. It was suicidal at night.

Henry wasn't done. "When we hear your plane, we turn on the lights. And call this phone so we can talk."

"Look, I'm not doing this. How about I just fly back to DC, and you drive Richard in one of the cars?"

Henry didn't respond. I heard a muffled conversation between the two then Richard was back on the phone.

"Daniel, you must fly me tonight. It be a matter of life and death. Henry and me we need something that I left in your plane.

We need it now! Daniel, you understand me?"

"No, God damn it, I don't understand you. You got yourself into this mess. I'm not going to kill myself trying to get you out of it. And, by the way, I know about the money you left in my plane."

There was a pause. "Daniel," he said slowly, "When I say it be a matter of life and death, I was not just talking about Henry and me. I am talking about you, you lovely wife, and you two little girls. Daniel, you need to tink about your family." His voice had dropped an octave. He had become a different, more dangerous, person.

"Daniel," he continued, "I be texting you some pictures. Call me back when you look at it. You got five minutes." The phone went dead. Was there an implied "or else" at the end of that sentence? A moment later his message arrived.

The subject line said, "See attached." The text said, "Call me quick." Three pictures were attached. The first was a picture of my house taken from across the street. The picture showed my wife's minivan sitting in its customary place in the driveway. From the angle of the sun, I estimated that the picture was taken during the early afternoon. A chill ran down my spine. *Did Richard have someone camped outside my house?*

The second picture showed my wife at our neighborhood supermarket, in the process of transferring plastic shopping bags from a grocery cart into the back seat of the minivan. She was alone. My heartbeat began to rise, The third picture made it stop. This time, the minivan was parked in front of the city skate park. Beth and Amy were clearly visible. Beth had her cell phone to her ear. My daughter was about to get in the side door. She was holding one arm with the other and had a pained expression on her face.

That son-of-a-bitch had my family under surveillance. Was my family being held captive? Are they safe? I was about to call the police and then stopped. What if someone with a gun was watching the house right now?

Then I panicked. Had five minutes passed? I pressed the redial button and called Richard.

"You bastard," I said before he could say anything, "you dirty, miserable son of a bitch. What have you done to my family? I'll kill you."

He ignored the insult with a laugh and said, "How do you feel?"

"I feel like killing you."

He laughed again. "Dat's good mon. Did you use the cocaine I give you?"

"No, I don't want any part of you, your filthy drugs, or money. What have you done to my family?"

"Daniel, you family be safe. I figure, you carrying my money, I need to make sure dat we are on the same team. You family be safe as long as we work together, me friend. So Daniel, will you use the cocaine?"

"No. Fuck you, Richard."

"But Daniel, you must use it. You must come wit da money and fly like you never fly before. We be waiting."

"You can just keep waiting. I'm not going to risk my life to help you. I never agreed to this."

"Daniel, you must trust me. Dere be people, very powerful people, I work with. You don't want anything bad to happen to you family. You can take ten thousand dollars extra for da trip."

That was convenient since I had already taken the money.

"What do you mean about something bad happening to my family?"

"Daniel, you must come. Come quickly."

The last was both a command and a plea all under the shadow of a threat. It was time to make a decision.

"I'm coming. Give me the location. I hope I don't crash."

"No problem, mon, you be a *good* pilot!" He read off the latitude and longitude numbers and repeated it twice just to make sure. As soon as we disconnected, my bowels turned into water. I rushed into the men's room again, this time for its intended purpose.

Afterward, I stared at myself in the mirror. This was the face that Beth married, the face that she looked at every day, the face that she trusted. Maybe she didn't trust me completely. Maybe she didn't share my love of flying. But she did count on me not to send killers to her front door. Self-disgust rose in my belly, and my vending machine dinner ended up in the toilet.

Then, as if I was a puppet controlled by another's hands, I snorted the cocaine. Richard was right. It did make me feel better.

I went outside to my plane, but before getting in, I stroked the engine and whispered, c*ome on baby, I know that landing was rough on you, but now I need you to come through for me again. I need you to come through for my family.*

When I called the tower for takeoff clearance the controller said, "Huh, tango the weather service predicts heavy turbulence. They recommend against flights by small aircraft."

"Tower, this is just a short relocation flight to the Ocean City, New Jersey airport. I won't have a problem."

"Ok, tango, taxi to runway 27. Permission granted to take off when ready. There's no traffic in the area."

An airplane is an awkward thing on the ground. It has no turn signals and no rearview mirrors. The wind makes things worse. The wings, the very thing that enables an airplane to fly are a hindrance on the ground. A stray gust can blow a light plane onto its back.

I tacked carefully to the start of the runway and took off quickly. Once off the ground, I turned south and had the Ocean City runway in sight in less than fifteen minutes. I radioed a warning to local aircraft that I was ready to land and made the required left-hand turns into the landing pattern.

My wheels met the asphalt a comfortable distance from the end of the runway, and I taxied slowly to a stop. If anyone was watching, I was just another airplane jockey landing for the night. The office that sold fuel and all the hangers were dark.

I turned off the engine and just sat on the apron, listings to the ticking of the cylinders as they cooled. Up to that moment, I had done nothing illegal. I could still fly home.

A new plan emerged. I would give half the money to the police. They would arrest Richard, and no one would be the wiser. But would we be safe? Maybe Richard had someone watching my house right now? Maybe he had connections within the police department?

My phone rang again. It was Richard.

"Daniel, where you be? We don't hear you?"

I took a deep breath and, at the moment, became an outlaw. "I'm on my way. I got delayed at Atlantic City."

"Please hurry mon. Please hurry."

I started the engine and taxied to the start of the runway with all my navigation lights and radios turned off. Once I was lined up on the centerline, I added power and was quickly airborne.

Besides violating countless FAA rules, I was invisible to other aircraft. I could kill other pilots and be killed. But the dye was cast.

The educated, analytical part of my brain said, "I'm doing this for my family." But there was another, baser motivation. It came from my gut. I was flying, and I was part of an adventure — Just me and my airplane against the world.

The airplane purchase was finally going to make sense. God damn it, I thought, I'm an outlaw. My heart beat faster. I sat up straighter. Biting my lip and with new resolve, I turned west into the blowing darkness.

***

When I got close, I called Henry's number. He picked up on the first ring. "Where you be?" he asked.

"I'm on my way, about eight miles out. Are the car lights on?"

"Yes, hurry mon."

When the GPS registered a half-mile out, I came down to five hundred feet. *I just hope there are no cell phone towers in the area.*

"We hear you mon, but we don't see you," Henry said.

I turned on my landing light, a single bright light on the right wing of the airplane. "We see you now," Henry said. At the same time, I saw the lights of the two cars. I passed over a row of trees towards the first one while dropping to three hundred feet. When the two cars were in line, I reduced the engine to idle, brought down the flaps and prayed.

I never saw the lone pine tree. *Why the hell didn't they tell me about the tree?* As I was lining up to land, a pine tree blocked my path. I had to turn away from the street to avoid it. But that maneuver cost altitude, and I was now less than one hundred feet above the cars and about fifty feet to the right of the road. I turned to the left and crossed the road at 30 feet and turned to the right again until I could see the headlights of the second car directly in front of me. First, the right wheel, then the left wheel and finally the nose wheel met the road with a familiar squeal.

I stood on the brakes with all my might. They locked, and I could smell burning rubber. Ignoring the smell, I tried to double the pressure. My speed diminished but so did the distance to the car. I was close enough to read the model name. It was a Mercury sedan. I got close enough to notice a dent in the left front bumper. Finally, the plane stopped ten feet away from disaster.

When the propeller stopped turning, I could hear Richard shouting, "You da man. You da man!"

I was proud of myself for keeping my head and getting down safely. I made a little plan to tell Beth about it and then realized that it was one triumph that I could never share with my wife.

Chapter 7

A Dark and Stormy Night

I sat strapped into my seat, shaking. *Did I really just land on a city street in the middle of the night?*

"Dat was some fancy flying," Richard shouted. I knew it was him because of his voice, but I couldn't see him because of the headlights. He banged on the door to shake me out of my stupor. Instead of a "thank you" or a hearty handshake, he ignored me and reached into the back to retrieve his bag and started to leave.

"No, you don't, you bastard. Give me that bag. You're going nowhere. Where do you get off, hiding drug money in my plane? Do you have someone watching my family?" We each held a strap and stared at each other. "Let go of the bag," I demanded.

"Daniel, I don't have time to talk. You family, safe. No one watches dem. I need di money, and I need to go. Henry's hurt."

Just then a gust of wind grabbed a wing. The plane rocked violently. "Henry can wait. Right now, I need your help. The money stays here." Richard nodded and released his grip.

Getting out, I tied a rope to the left wing and said, "Richard, take this and find an anchor. Look for something heavy." If we didn't get it secured, it'd flip over.-

I ran around to the right side and, with some effort, was able to tie that wing to a storm grate. That helped. Searching in the dark, I found a cement block and used it to anchor the tail. That should have kept the plane secure, but it still jumped like a frog with each gust of wind.

Three ropes should have steadied the plane, why was it still twitching like a three-year- old getting a beating? Because one two ropes were secured. The rope I assigned to Richard, still flapped in the breeze. My co-conspirator left me in the lurch again.

Typical Richard, I thought as I retrieved a stake and hammer from my tool box, he disappears when most needed. I had a sinking feeling about the bag of money but had no time to do anything about it.

I walked the loose rope to the curb just as a bolt of lightning and a roll of thunder heralded the start of the rain. It quickly became a downpour. I knelt in the wet grass and pounded the stake into the ground using more force than necessary. In my mind, the head of the stake morphed into Richard's smiling face. Take that. Pow! And that! Pow!

By the third blow, I could tell that someone was watching me but didn't look up assuming it was Richard.

"What happened?" I asked, "Why didn't you secure the wing like I asked you to?" There was no response. That just made me madder, and I hit the stake yet again.

I secured the rope to the stake and got up brushing the mud off my soaking pants. That's when I realized the person standing next to me was neither Richard nor Henry, but a large man holding a gun. And the gun was pointed at my chest.

"Get down on your knees!"

His face was hidden in the shadows. His voice carried the long vowels of a New Jersey native.

I stepped forward intending to comply with his command. That's when my right ankle caught the rope. I tripped, and as I fell, I instinctively extended my hand to break my fall. Halfway to the ground, my hammer hit his forearm. He screamed and dropped the gun. My knees hit the pavement, and my pants ripped.

"Son of a bitch!" The man joined me on the ground, scrambling for his weapon. I slipped on the wet surface. My right foot connected with his gun sending it skidding away into the darkness. That's when the heavens really opened up.

The rain was so thick, we two combatants could hardly see each other. I started shivering from the sudden cold. Then, as if to accompany the deep bass of the thunder, came the higher pitched sound of a gunshot.

The storm created only brief intermission to our macabre ballet. The man tried to kick and missed. I swung out blindly with my hammer. It connected with the man's right knee. He fell on his back.

"Son of a bitch!" He tried to get up, but hit his head on the wing, and fell a second time.

I smiled, certain my plane had joined the fight on my behalf. As much as I wanted to, I couldn't run away. I had to fight for the first time in my life. I had to protect my plane, just as my plane had protected me.

I tightened my grip on the hammer and hit him again, this time aiming at his left knee. His kneecap shattered with a satisfying crack. He screamed again, but his scream was overshadowed by a louder scream from the other side of the car. The screamer had a Jamaican accent. Then I heard a second gunshot.

"Tony," my assailant yelled, "Tony, come help!" Thunder crashed over our confrontation, drowning out his appeal.

He crawled towards the car trying to get away from me. I knew I had to stop him. A dark and scary part of my brain took over. I used my hammer to hit him in the back of his head. If I was going to die, I thought, it's *not* going to be in a half-finished housing development in rural New Jersey.

He continued to crawl away from me. Then I hit him again

in almost the same spot, this time using all my strength. The head of the hammer dented his skull. Blood came out in a modest flow. He stopped moving.

"Stay down," I commanded. There was no response.

He lay face-down in the gutter. Blood added a crimson hue to the water on its way to the storm grate. I dropped the hammer and knelt by him. *Did I kill him?*

Getting as close as I dared, I was able to hear his breathing. It came in shallow, ragged bursts. He was still alive. A shudder ran down my spine, and if I weren't soaking wet, I would have felt the sweat break out of every pore.

Until that night, I had never been in a physical fight in my life. I never played football, never wrestled. That night some primordial part of my DNA took over. The DNA, not I, smashed the hammer into the man's skull. A moment later remorse replaced rage. *I have to find Richard and get this guy to a hospital.*

I used plastic ties to secure the man's hands and ankles. Then, with the help of my flashlight, I found the gun right on the edge of a storm drain. Before doing anything else, I checked the inside of my plane. As I suspected, the money was gone.

"Follow the money" is always good advice. With the gun in my hand, I came around the car and found the bag next to Richard. My friend was on his knees facing a large man, presumably Tony. Tony held a pistol to Richard's forehead.

I took a step forward. Tony sensed my presence and said, "Did the pilot give you any trouble?" It was my turn to talk, but I didn't know what to say. Should I try to imitate a New Jersey accent, and pretend to be his partner? Should I say "drop the gun we have you surrounded?" Should I offer to trade the money for Richard's life?

I said nothing and my lack of response gave me away. Tony looked at me and moved his aim from Richard to me. Tutored by a thousand Hollywood scripts, I raised mine and said, "gun."

Tony smiled. I got angry and thrust my arm forward. Somehow the wrong finger touched the trigger in the right way. The gun fired. Tony yelled, dropped his gun and fell on top of Richard. There was a moment when I couldn't tell who I had hit.

Tony stayed down clutching his thigh. Richard emerged, without hesitating, fired two bullets through Tony's forehead. He turned to me with a savage look on his face. That's when I first saw the huge gash on the right side of his head. His shoulder was covered in blood.

"Where di other?"

"He's back near the plane on the street. I tied him up. He can't hurt us. Please don't kill him."

"You tie 'im up?"

"Yeah. It was an accident."

"Jus by accident, you tie up a mon?"

"Well, I hit him with a hammer first."

"Daniel, Daniel, Daniel. I tink you woulda do good inna dis bizness."

I smiled and said, "I don't think so. Where's Henry?"

"Henry's over dere. See if you can help him. I'll be right back."

Richard went around the car. I walked over to a pile of darkness that once was Henry. He was beyond help. He died holding a large black duffel bag, identical to the one that had been in my plane.

Two more shots rang out in the diminishing rain. Did Richard kill the other man or did the other man get loose and kill Richard? Or were they both dead?

A figure came out of the headlights. Not a figure really, just a shadow in the brightness surrounded by darkness. Was it Richard? I raised my pistol. The silhouette raised its hands. "Hey, Daniel, please don't kill me. Me hurt enough already." Then he laughed — in the middle of the macabre night, Richard laughed his jolly "no problem" laugh. And I laughed with him. Somehow I saw the humor in this major fuck-up of a drug deal. We were a bizarre and dark version of a *Laurel and Hardy* comedy.

Maybe, it was all a bad, practical joke. At any moment the three men will get up and join in the laughter. It wasn't blood, I tried to reason, it was ketchup. Maybe it was all just a horrible, tasteless, practical joke.

Then I stopped laughing. The dead didn't get up. The red stuff was blood, not ketchup.

Oh, my God, Richard had just killed a defenseless man. I felt sick.

"How's Henry?" Richard asked.

"Henry's dead." I dropped the gun and sank to my knees. It was all coming back to me. In the space of about thirty minutes, I landed illegally on a residential street, beat a man into unconsciousness, shot a gun for the first time in my life, and witnessed three murders.

I threw up for the second time that night, and whatever was left in my stomach covered the gun and splattered my pants. *What the fuck am I doing here? I want to go home!*

Richard confirmed Henry's condition. Then, he sat on the curb under the shelter of a wing and watched Henry's unmoving body. I watched the rain dripping off Richard's dreadlocks.

We move to the nearby car. Carefully maneuvering around my airplane, Richard drove to the other end of our makeshift runway and the Ford Explorer. Most of my concentration was on my innards — I didn't want to throw up in the car.

Richard put the car in park. "Dis is how it is. Dem two guys, dem was supposed to bring us di cocaine, and den we give dem the money. We do dis maybe once a month for di past few months. And every month dem two guys short us on di cocaine. And when I bring it back to me boss, 'im take it outta my share. So dis time, we change di money."

"What do you mean, you changed the money?"

"You'll see. You drive di other car back an' I'll show you."

"Before you show me anything, before I help you, I need to know what you did to my family."

"Daniel, like me tell you, you family safe. Henry, 'im take di pictures. I'll show you."

We drove back to the plane and parked the cars on the grass. Richard opened the SUV's tailgate to create a temporary roof for the work we had to do. He sat in the back and pressed a Philadelphia Eagles t-shirt against his head to stem the flow. Then he lit a cigarette and gave me orders.

"We hav' tree bag. One dat was inna you plane, one by Henry and one more inna di other car. Bring dem here. Also, bring me Henry's phone an' him wallet."

Getting the things from Henry was difficult. His lifeless arms cradled the bag against his lifeless chest as if it were a living thing. When I lifted him up, he stared at me with accusing eyes.

The second bag, the one that Richard had in my plane, was on the ground not far from Henry.

I found the third bag in the back seat of the sedan. When I was done, three identical black duffle bags filled the back of the Ford Explorer. The rain storm had moved away leaving only an annoying drizzle.

"Okay Richard, tell me about my family."

"It be real simple. Henry 'im drive 'im car to the Cape May Ferry inna di morning, and 'im wait by you house. Den 'im follow you wifey and take the pictures. Look inna 'im phone. 3698 ah di password."

I opened the phone and looked at the saved pictures. The time stamps confirmed that they were taken in the early afternoon that day.

"How do I know you don't have anyone else watching my family?

"Daniel, you nuh know. You must trustt me."

"So what's in the bags?"

"Open di first bag and tell me what inna it."

"It's full of glassine envelopes. I assume it's cocaine."

"Dat's right mon. Itta very good cocaine. Each packet ah one gram and it worth four hundred dollars on di street if we nuh cut it. We talk about all a dat later. Ah, three thousand of dem packets less a few I take and one I give to you. Open di next bag. Tell me what you see."

 "It's the bag that you hid in my plane. It's full of money."

"Right again mon. It full ah hundred dollar bill. Every bundle have one hundred bills. Ah, one hundred and sixteen of dem bundles we have. T'was one hundred and twenty when we started but me an Henry, we tek four."

I didn't tell him that he was one short. The bag now had one hundred and fifteen bundles. I kept a straight face. Richard when on, "Now open di third one."

"It's the same. It's filled with money."

"Open ah bundle."

I removed the rubber band and spread out the bills on the tailgate. The outside bills, the ones used as wrappers, displayed the now-familiar picture of Benjamin Franklyn. But the remaining ninety-eight bills were ones.

"Holy shit, you were going to cheat on the payment. What do you call this?"

Richard smiled. "We call dis a Jamaican sandwich. We not cheatn, we just ah get back what dem tek from us. Every ting was going good until di big guy dat you buss up, 'im open di bag with di money and look pon di bills. Den everything went to shit when Henry try shot 'im and miss. Dey shoot him and den beat me up. You save mi life."

***

We were quiet for a while. Richard squirmed trying to find a comfortable position. Every time he moved, he groaned. Finally, he reached into the first bag one and extracted one of the envelopes.

"Tek some ah dis."

I didn't argue. We both took a hit. It cleared my head, and my hands stopped shaking. It had the same effect on my companion. He stopped groaning, at least for a while, but his increased heart rate made his head wound bleed again. The t-shirt was soaked. I found a flannel jacket in the backseat of the other car and gave it to my companion to use as a compress.

"How badly are you hurt?" I asked.

 Richard chuckled. "Mi hurt all over. Dat Tony guy kick me inna mi side. Tink me ribs is broken. Den him hit me on da head wid him gun."

"You'll need stitches."

"Ya mon, maybe we can find a needle and thread inna you toolbox."

I didn't have a needle and thread. Even if it had, I wouldn't know how to stitch a scalp. But I did have duct tape. The duct tape worked to bind Richard's chest.

Richard closed all three bags, and I put them in the back of the plane. Then we lifted the bodies into the SUV with the help creating a ramp I created using two boards from a half-finished house.

I drove the Explorer trying not to think about my cargo. Richard drove the other car. Our little caravan of death left the development and headed west. The pavement ended after a few blocks, but we continued on a dirt road further and further into the pinewood forest. Finally, the road ended at an informal trash dump.

I pointed my flashlight at the SUV's back quarter panel.

Richard aimed and fired three bullets near the gas cap. The third one hit its target releasing a thin stream of unleaded onto the road.

We made a fuse by soaking newspaper in the gas then lighting it with Richard's Bic. I threw it into the puddle, and the gasoline ignited with a whoosh. We watched until the back left tire exploded then returned to the scene of the crimes.

It was after 3:00 am. The rain was a damp memory. Above us, the sky was mostly clear with silver clouds sailing past an almost full moon. I couldn't help comparing the moon's orderly, monthly orbit with my suddenly chaotic life. Why couldn't my life be as well regulated? Yet I knew that, ultimately, I was the cause of the chaos.

In spite of the chaos, I never felt more alive. In many ways, I was very fortunate. My parents stayed together until they died. We always had enough money. Following a path set before me, I stumbled through college, graduate school, marriage, fatherhood and my first job. I did what was expected and got the expected results. Until that night, I never faced existential demands. That is the thrill of being a pilot. The only thing between life and death is luck and your innate skill.

"Richard, stay in the car and for God's sake, keep that jacket pressed against your head." He nodded and closed his eyes.

I turned the plane around and pulled it back to the very end of the road. The moonlight shining off the wet pavement made the street easy to see.

Getting Richard out of the car and into the plane was more difficult. I moved the car onto the grass and as close to right wing as I dared. "Richard, wake up. We have to go."

It seemed that the drive to the garbage dump absorbed all of Richard's strength. I half-carried him to the open door of the plane, but there was no way I could lift him into the seat. I placed his right arm on a grab bar and said, "Richard, for God's sake, you need to pull." From somewhere deep inside, he found the strength to get aboard.

I was ready to leave, but Richard stopped me. "Daniel, you need to burn da otta car mon."

"Why?"

"Because, Daniel, me blood an you fingerprints be all over da car. Jus tak it dare an burn it." He handed me one of the guns. "Tak dis. You know wat ta do."

At first, I thought about parking the car at the end of the street as a flaming marker. But that would destroy my night vision. So I burned the car onto the concrete pad that would someday be the floor of a two-car garage.

Back at the airplane, I pressed firmly on the brake pedals, lowered the flaps, set the propeller to maximum pitch, then started the engine and pushed the throttle all the way in. I watched the RPM gauge climb up to and just above the red line. Then I released the brakes.

We were rolling. I kept my eye on the right-hand curb, illuminated by the moon and my landing light. At the same time, I watched my airspeed. I needed at least sixty miles per hour for takeoff.

The airspeed needle was at fifty when a set of headlights appeared on the road to our left. My eyes swerved to the intruder but quickly returned to the pine trees at the end of the street.

"Someone's coming!" Richard yelled and pulled out his gun. I ignored him, focusing instead on the airspeed indicator. I gripped the yoke with white knuckles and forced myself not to pull it up.

When the needle moved up to fifty-five, I said, "Fuck it," and I pulled back on the yoke. We were airborne. But we were just airborne. I knew that if I pulled back too far and tried to climb over the trees, we would stall and drop like a stone. If I didn't and kept the yoke steady, we would crash into the trees.

I opted for a compromise. I raised the flaps halfway, trading lift for airspeed, and turned slightly to the left, heading directly towards the perpendicular road and the on-coming car. We flew over it with about forty feet to spare. I used the clear space over the road to gain enough airspeed to bring the flaps all the way up and then gained more altitude.

We were on our way. But someone had seen us. Were they able to see the numbers on the side of my plane?

I turned off my landing light and stayed just above the treetops as I headed southwest.

There was no way I could get back to the Gaithersburg airport without getting clearance from air traffic control. I needed a plausible story.

My solution was the airport in Millsboro, New Jersey, just east of the Delaware River. If I could fly there undetected, I could contact ATC, pretend to be an early morning commuter, and get the necessary codes. It was a good plan, but one that would only succeed if no one witnessed our arrival at Millsboro.

I explained my plan to Richard but got no response. He was asleep with the bloody flannel pressed to the side of his head.

The clock on my dashboard said that it was four in the morning. The whole encounter had taken about five hours.

I turned off the engine about a half-mile from the airport. My piston-powered airplane became an overweight glider.

My flight instructor's voice invaded my head. "You can gain speed by losing altitude or maintain altitude by losing speed. The trick is to start your glide at the correct height and distance from the runway." I was hoping that I started high enough.

Richard woke up when the engine stopped.

"Holy shit, di engine stop. We going to die?"

"Not yet, Richard, I won't kill you, not today."

The ground beneath us was littered with stumps, tree trunks, and construction equipment. The airport, it seemed, was in the process of extending the runway. We would die for sure if we landed short.

The end of the runway was still three hundred feet away. I had my hand on the ignition key ready to start the engine if needed. I wanted to land undetected, but that was less important than landing safely.

Our speed dropped too quickly, so I lowered the nose to increase speed, but that cost me altitude. Finally, the gods of aviation took pity on me. My seat of the pants calculations worked. We flew over the airport fence with less than a dozen feet to spare and landed on the first few yards of asphalt.

The moonlight shining into the cabin reflected off Richard's wide grin. "You da man! You da man!" he said for the third and fourth time that night.

I had no snappy comeback. I sat there without talking and waited until my knees stopped shaking.

I found a bottle of water, purchased three days earlier, tucked behind the passenger seat. It was warm, but I didn't care. I needed every drop. It calmed me. I took a deep breath then started the engine and turned on all lights and radios.

"Philly ATC this is Cessna N-two-three-five-tango at Millsboro airport requesting transit through your area en route to Gaithersburg, Maryland."

"Roger, Cessna, permission granted. Climb and maintain 2000 feet direct flight granted."

The airways were empty that morning. The moon, edging towards the horizon provided a silver highway as we crossed the Delaware Bay.

A friendly female voice from Baltimore ATC took over when we crossed into Maryland, and she vectored me directly over BWI airport — something that would never happen during daylight hours. I saw only one or two baggage carts moving on the tarmac.

My feelings on the return trip were in stark opposition to my euphoria on the eastward flight. No longer the king of the air, I was a wet, tired, and bruised assistant drug transporter. I wanted to fly and make money doing it, but three murders and an illegal landing were too much.

We landed without incident and taxied to my previous spot on the apron. "Richard, we're down." I shook my passenger awake.

"Yah, mon, dats good," he said in a very groggy voice. I half-carried him again, this time to the passenger seat of his car and went back to get the three bags and my computer case.

When I got back to the car, Richard was snoring. He smelled of gunpowder, blood, and gasoline. I realized that I must smell the same way or worse. Once we were on the road, the open window revived him. "Where we going?"

"I'm taking you to a hospital."

"No way mon, hospitals, dem ask too many questions. How me a go explain dis?" he said pointing to his head.

He was right. I shook my head and tuned the radio to a local station. The announcer let us know that it was five a.m. and that the rain the previous night had measured a welcome half inch. There were no reports of traffic tie-ups on the roads. "It's Wednesday, hump day," he proclaimed, "have a humpy day."

Back at the Marriott, I parked far away from the entrance and reluctantly gave Richard the car keys.

"Daniel, I can't drive you to work today," he said.

My God, work! I had forgotten all about it.

"Look" he continued, "you take the bags. Half the money is yours. Hold onto mi money and di blow, and I'll link you when I get better. You did great, mon."

He opened the cocaine stash and extracted a handful of the packets to refill his pockets before handing the duffle to me with one hand and two packets with the other. "Dem two ah fe you.

Dat'll help you get through wid di day." I had to help him stand.

"Richard, are you okay to drive?" The blood had turned his shirt into crimson cardboard. When he moved, the shirt cracked and little flecks of dried blood fell to the ground.

"Mi alright," he said as he got behind the wheel.

I was about to close the door, but Richard stopped me. He found a pencil and one of his business cards. He wrote something on the back and handed it to me. It had the name "Ronnie" followed by a post office box address and phone number. One corner was embossed with Richard's bloody thumbprint.

"Dis ah mi sista inna Kingston. If something happens to me, get rid ah di blow and give her mi share." I nodded and put his card in my wallet. I was ready to go, but he grabbed my arm. 'Member Daniel, money come and go but family a di most important thing. Take care ah you family." Then he drove away.

I dragged my new luggage into the hotel just as the sun emerged over the horizon.

Chapter 8

Dan's Fortune

The mirrored elevator door reflected the rigors of my long night. There were holes in the knees of my pants, and my cuffs were torn. The black, nylon flying jacket that my wife gave me for my last birthday was now a wet rag. Any article of clothing still intact was soaked — from without by the rain and from within by my perspiration. I only hoped I could salvage my muddy shoes.

All my clothes, even my underwear, went into a plastic laundry bag for later disposal. The shower washed off the brown New Jersey mud. Next, a mixture of blood, both pheasant, and human, turned the water a pale pink. Finally, my sphincter muscles released an internal flood adding a yellow hue to the spiral as it headed for the drain.

If only the water would wash away my memories. The man I hit with my hammer haunted me. Why did I hit him a second time? If Richard had not administered his coup de grace and the man had survived, he would be horribly maimed for life. I was a murderer.

I tried to reason that it was in self-defense. But I knew, deep down, that there was something else in play. Some dark part of my psyche, a part that I had suppressed for four decades, emerged and delivered the blows. In so many ways it was an act of revenge, not at my assailant, but in retaliation for incidents in my childhood. The Christmas parties I wasn't invited to because I was Jewish. Bam! The girls who didn't return my phone calls. Bam! My mother's indifference. Bam! Bam! Bam!

Maybe I was an outlaw? If I'm an outlaw, the usual rules don't apply to me. I killed a man with a hammer. I violated FAA rules. I'm hiding stolen money and drugs.

Even after rinsing and repeating twice, the smell of burning bodies stayed in my hair.

I dressed in spare clothes and wrote a list of things I had to do. First and foremost, I had to find a way to secure the bags of money and drugs. Second, I had to make sure Richard was all right. At the bottom of the list was "contact Richard's sister." I looked at the last item then crossed it out.

I tried to leave the room, and get breakfast before going to work, but the duffle bags blocked my way. They blocked the hallway leading to the door like uninvited guests at a wedding party.

I had no idea how to deal with the bag containing the gun and drugs, so I consigned it, unopened, to the bottom of the closet.

In spite of my growling stomach, I spilled the contents of the money bags onto the bed and separated the hundred-dollar bills from the singles, then I counted and re-bagged the mess. I did the same with the bag holding only hundred-dollar bills.

All told, there was just under $620,000 in cash. Half of it was mine. It was enough to fund my family comfortably for six or eight years. Maybe longer if I invested it wisely.

I didn't consider the value of the cocaine. That was going back to Richard untouched and as soon as possible. I was scared of the drugs. I could almost smell them. They were bait. I knew that they would attract people who would do anything to get them.

I stacked the money bags on top of the cocaine in the closet and closed the door. Walking to the elevator, I realized that I was so naive. The previous evening I'd risked my life for forty of those hundred-dollar bills. Now the hotel closet sequestered three hundred times that amount, plus a fortune in cocaine. I had to come up with a plan.

The elevator was empty when I got on. When it stopped at the second floor, Maria entered, and the analytical part of my brain went on vacation.

She was dressed in black, tailored slacks and a short-sleeved, purple blouse, looking every bit the successful businesswoman in casual attire. She wore her beautiful, jet black hair pulled back in a neat bun. I could see that it was secured with an antique-looking silver clip adding an exotic element to her appearance.

She smiled and said, "Hello Dan, are you ready for another day of teaching? You look a little tired." Unconsciously, I passed my hand through my hair with one hand and surreptitiously checked my fly with the other.

"Morning, Maria. Yes, I think I'm ready. I'm a little tired. I didn't sleep much last night."

"Why's that," she asked with a smile.

"I had to fly a friend to New Jersey. A storm came through, and we had to wait until it dissipated. We got back late." I realized that I was babbling. I hadn't felt this nervous talking to a woman since high school.

We stood there, about three feet apart, watching the elevator doors close. We didn't say anything else. I felt a magnetic force pulling me to her. All my plans, all the urgency I felt a few minutes ago, evaporated. I wanted to get closer but didn't dare.

We joined the line of guests waiting for tables at the restaurant. When the hostess asked, "Are you two together?" Maria took control and said, "Yes."

I ordered a three-egg omelet, bacon, hash brown potatoes and extra toast. Maria was content with one poached egg and a bowl of cut fruit. After my first substantial bites, I asked, "What did you do last night?"

"It was very boring. I went over reports, watched TV and went to sleep." She drank her coffee and looked at me with those deep, dark eyes. "I think I dreamed about you," she said with a shy, blushing smile.

I blushed in response. "You dreamed about me? I dreamt about you on Monday night."

"Only Monday night? What about last night?"

I didn't have an answer that I could share. So I just smiled.

"Dan, I believe that you and I will become good friends," she said. "I still remember my dream. Would you like to hear it?"

Every fiber of my body screamed *yes*! Then I looked at my watch. It was already 8:30. I needed to get to work.

"Maria, I need to ask you for a favor. Can you drive me to work today? I'm teaching at the Parklawn building in Rockville, just off the beltway, about a half-hour from here. And can you pick me up at noon and drive me to the Enterprise car rental office. It's just a few blocks from here. I'll buy you lunch, and we can talk about our dreams."

"What happened to your taxi driver?"

"He's sick today."

Maria consulted her smartphone and then looked up with a quizzical smile. "I'll do it if you agree to do a favor for me."

"Anything, Maria. I'll be happy to do anything." My dirty mind began thinking of things I could do for her.

"Be careful, Dan, you don't know me." She looked up from her phone and stared at me the same way my wife would examine the qualities of a cantaloupe at the supermarket. I held my breath. "Anyway," she continued, "my boss is hosting a dinner for clients tonight, and I don't have a date. Will you come with me?" I remembered to breathe again.

"Yes, of course. Do I need to get dressed up?"

"What you're wearing would be fine except — do you have

a tie?"

"No, I stopped wearing one years ago." She made a face registering her disappointment.

"That's okay I guess. My boss will pick us up at seven."

I gulped the last of my coffee. "I need to go back to my room for a moment to get my briefcase. Can we meet in ten minutes?"

I left her at the table checking her emails. I scanned the other women in the dining room and concluded that I ate breakfast with the most beautiful one there.

Back in my room, I took a deep breath and pressed the blinking button on the hotel telephone. There were three messages, all from my wife. I called her cell phone, and she picked up on the first ring. "Where the hell have you been?"

"Beth, look, it's a long story."

"I don't have time for a story. I'm on the way to the hospital with Amy."

My world collapsed. I could feel the sweat forming on my forehead and in my recently washed armpits. The large breakfast began to turn in my stomach.

"What happened? What's wrong with Amy?"

"She went skateboarding yesterday afternoon. A boy bumped into her when she was using the half pipe. She fell hard on her arm. She was crying when she called me. Luckily I was nearby, shopping. I thought it was just a bruise, so I put ice on it and gave her a Tylenol, but she had a terrible night. She's in lots of pain. This morning her arm is swollen to the size of a pumpkin. Why didn't you call last night?"

"I left you a message. I had to fly a client to New Jersey. We got stuck at an airport because of the weather, and I didn't get back until very late. Is Amy all right?"

"You and your fucking airplane! I don't know if she's all right. I'm pulling into the emergency entrance now."

"Let me talk to Amy."

"Forget it. We have to go. I'll call you later."

The phone went dead. My heart sank even lower.

***

Maria's car slowed to a crawl as soon as we entered the beltway. "There must have been an accident," she said. I paid little attention. I was thinking about my daughter. I remembered the pictures on Henry's phone. One showed Beth with her cell phone to her ear. Another showed Beth at the skate park holding Amy's arm as she got into the minivan.

"Are you going to be late?" Maria asked. "What time does your class start?"

"I'm already late, but that's okay. My assistant is teaching this morning's session." Frankly, I didn't give a damn. *Why was I still working? I had just become a half-millionaire. Why don't I just ditch it all and fly home?*

Maria tuned the radio to a local station to get the traffic report. "We are just getting word about the accident on the northern beltway. There are reports of multiple injuries and one possible fatality. Only one lane of the beltway is open. Authorities advise commuters to use alternative routes."

My wife called as we crept along.

"Well, she's scheduled for surgery. She has a broken arm." Beth paused for a moment and then continued with a sob in her voice. "The doctor says it's a clean break, she'll be okay. She'll be in a cast for the rest of the summer — so much for swimming. Where are you? Why aren't you teaching?"

"I'm on the Beltway trying to get to class. There was an accident, and all but one lane is blocked. Does the doctor think that there'll be a problem with her arm after it heals?"

"No, he says that she'll be fine. Dan, I had to write a check for the co-pay when we registered. It was for one-hundred-and-fifty dollars. Will it be OK?"

"Don't worry, it'll be fine. I deposited my government check yesterday." Meanwhile, I visualized the stacks of hundred hundred-dollar bills in my closet.

Just as Beth and I were saying goodbye, it was Maria's turn to pass the wrecks. First, I saw the cement truck and then another car, both with minor damage. Then I saw a black Cadillac. The whole front end was smashed in. The front door was missing, probably torn off the car by the firemens' Jaws of Life tool.

It had to be Richard's car. Even with the damage, I recognized the faded roof and the signature headlight held in place with duct tape. If there were any doubt, I saw the fresh scratches along its right side and the broken right side mirror.

A body lay on the road covered by a white sheet. The paramedics were getting ready to load it into an ambulance.

Maria noted my concern. "Dan, what's wrong?

"The taxi driver you saw me with yesterday morning. That's his car. I'm sure of it."

"Oh, my God, so the body they're loading right now . . ."

I couldn't find my voice for a moment. "Yes, it must be him."

"Dan, I'm so sorry. How well did you know him?"

"Not well. We just met this week. He's the person I flew with to New Jersey last night. We had our ups and downs, but he always made me laugh. Most of the time I was laughing at myself."

Why did I let him drive? He had lost so much blood. Now, what will I do? Before that moment, I had the fantasy that I would give a recovered Richard his bags, and he would give me a cashier's check for six hundred thousand dollars. "Here you be, mon. Thanks for your good work. Goodbye and don't worry so much."

In that fantasy, I would pay off all the credit cards, buy Beth a new car, make substantial contributions to the girls' college funds and invest the remainder into growth-oriented mutual funds.

All those plans, hopes, and dreams vanished in that pile of twisted metal on the beltway. *What do I do about the cocaine? And what about that car that saw us in New Jersey last night?*

I realized that Richard, by dying, had forever inserted himself into my life.

When I finally got there, the class was already in session. I took a seat in the back of the room with the full intention of taking notes. But the room was warm. I was tired. My pen stopped moving. I drifted off thinking about my daughter, her broken arm, the white-sheet-covered body, the twisted metal on the highway, and the murders.

The sound of chairs scraping the floor woke me. It was noon. I approached Michelle saying, "You did a great job."

Her face took on a very stern look. "How would you know? You were sleeping."

"Not really. I might have closed my eyes, but ... "

"Dan, we heard you snore."

I was caught and tried to wiggle out of it. "My daughter broke her arm, so I was up most of the night." Suddenly lying had become easy for me.

"I'm sure that you're doing a great job." My hand found my to-do list in my pocket. "Can you teach the rest of the class today? I have a bunch of errands to do and, as you know, my contract for the remaining classes this year is canceled."

Michelle looked concerned. She opened the textbook to the next lesson and flipped the pages. Finally, she said, "Sure, I'll do it. Will you teach tomorrow?"

"Certainly, you can count on it." I tried making my voice sound enthusiastic.

I called Beth as I headed to the elevator. "Has Amy had her surgery?"

"No, they admitted her, but they're waiting for an available operating room. The surgeon came in and showed me the x-rays.

It looks like a clean break, but what do I know? They gave Amy something for the pain. She's sleeping. Sara's with her. Where are you?"

"I'm on my way to lunch. I wish I could be there."

"I do too. Call me later. She should be out of surgery by five."

***

Maria and her car were at the curb when I emerged from the building.

"How's your daughter?" she asked as I got into her car.

"She's at the hospital, awaiting surgery. She'll be fine. I should be there."

"Did you hear anything about your friend?"

"No."

We found an old fashioned diner a few doors away from the car rental office. Maria climbed the entrance steps ahead of me, and despite everything else in my life, I couldn't help staring at her behind. With every step, her slacks revealed an outline of her underwear. *Will I ever get to see that lingerie?*

My companion carried the bulk of the conversation as she ate her chicken caesar salad. I watched intently as she dipped a piece of lettuce in the dressing and transferred it to her mouth. To my delight, a bit of white escaped and took residence on her upper lip. I mimed touching my own lip. She blushed, adding a bit of pink to her light brown complexion. Then a long, very red tongue reached up and captured the errant morsel.

With a naughty twinkle in her eyes, she isolated a small piece of chicken. Making sure I watched, she dipped it in the dressing and slowly brought it to her lips. The spear of white meat stayed in a holding pattern near those lips and that tongue while she chewed, all the while staring intently at my face.

Excited, my eyes shifted from her face to the meat on the fork, then back again. Would she eat it now? Would she wait?

Then, I'm certain just to tease me, she dipped the meat into the dressing a second time. Again she brought it close to her mouth in slow motion. Her tongue came out. Would she grab it like a frog capturing a fly? My heartbeat quickened. I began to sweat despite the air conditioning. My world contracted. I was totally focused on her mouth, her fork and the piece of poultry about to be sacrificed to the god of lust.

Her tongue took on a life of its own. It grabbed the meat from the fork in midair and lured it into that sweet cavity. The lips closed. Her jaw muscles took over.

Smiling in a very self-satisfied way, she finished her performance with a drink of water and rested her folk on her plate. Was she done? I wanted more.

Maria chuckled, "Dan, are you okay? You seem to be sweating."

I fled to the men's room to wash my face. When I returned, Maria was impatiently checking her cell phone. "Dan, I have to get going. Are you sure you'll be all right? Don't forget, we have a dinner date tonight — seven p.m. sharp." She left planting an air-kiss in the vicinity of my cheek as she passed.

I sat for a while as my heartbeat returned to normal then walked to the car rental office where I selected a mid-sized sedan with a large trunk.

I found a branch of my bank and handed the teller 50 of the hundred dollar bills, covered with a deposit slip. I was certain that she was going to ask questions about the provenance of the money, but, thankfully our conversation was limited to the weather and the traffic on Wisconsin Avenue.

My next stop was my hotel. A business-oriented hotel is a quiet place in the middle of the day. My room was freshly serviced. No gunmen with ugly grins were waiting for me on the furniture. It took two trips to get the three duffle bags into the trunk of the car. All that cash and drugs were heavy.

A short drive up Wisconsin Avenue found a small regional bank. There I opened a new checking account using $5,000 as my initial deposit. I was ready with a long story about a small inheritance, but the vice president (they're all vice presidents) asked no questions outside of the usual name and address. As an afterthought, I inquired about safe deposit boxes. "We only have the very large boxes left," he said.

I stuffed a handful of the singles and $10,000 in hundreds in my computer case. The rest went into the box. The bag of drugs stayed in the trunk of the car. It was destined for a watery grave. I wanted to handle it as little as possible.

I considered stopping at a department store to replace my ruined clothes but didn't. I was exhausted and tired and confused in a way I had never before experienced.

Back at my hotel room, I didn't open my computer or check my phone messages. I simply undressed to my underwear, fell onto the bed, and drifted into a sound and dreamless sleep.

Chapter 9

What a night

Maria's call woke me. "Hi Dan, are you ready?"

"Err … I was just taking a nap."

"Dan, you didn't forget, did you? We're having dinner with my boss tonight. You're still coming aren't you?" Her voice had a pleading, whining tone.

Suddenly everything clicked into place. "Yes, of course, I'll meet you in the lobby in twenty minutes."

"Please hurry. We can't be late."

I washed my face then called my wife. "How's Amy?"

"The surgery went well. She's sleeping. They gave her something for the pain. They put a big cast on her arm. It's white and as big as one of her legs." She paused. "I wish you were here."

"I do too. How's Sara taking it?"

"Suddenly she gets to be the big sister again. You know how Amy overshadows Sara. Now Sara has a chance to be in charge. She's already cleaned Amy's room and has started making lists of thing they can do together this summer even with the cast. How's the teaching going?"

"The class is fine. I have a good group this time. I'm going out to dinner tonight with a potential new client. I think it'll turn into something substantial."

"Lucky you — I've been eating in the hospital cafeteria." She paused, and I could tell that she had her hand on the microphone.

"Dan, I have to go. The doctor needs to talk to me. Bye."

I put the phone down. *I really should be there.*

Someone knocked on the door. I heart leaped in my chest. *The cops? The cartel?* Three more knocks. "Who is it?"

"It's Maria. Are you decent?"

Only a pair of white jockey shorts separated me from nakedness. "One minute, please." I hurriedly dressed in my wrinkled pants and a clean t-shirt.

When I opened the door, I found a woman transformed. No longer wearing the slacks and short sleeve blouse, she now wore a navy skirt suit and a cream-colored silk top. Silver hoops dangled from her ears. Silver bangles clinked from her right wrist. In contrast to her unadorned appearance during the day, she had enhanced her face with eyeliner, blush, and lipstick. She carried a shopping bag with the Macy's logo.

She looked me over much in the same way that a butcher might examine a questionable cut of meat. "What were you planning on wearing tonight?" she asked with a scowl. Without waiting for my reply, she opened the closet. Her fingers flipped through my few shirts and one jacket like a disappointed shopper at a used clothing store.

"I thought so. You have nothing. Here, I bought you some things. I think I got the right size." She emptied the Macy's bag onto the bed and showed me an expensive pale blue long-sleeved shirt with French cuffs, a small box containing a pair of plain gold cufflinks, and a striped silk tie.

"Maria, you didn't have to shop for me."

"Actually, I did. I can't have you showing up looking like a homeless man I found on the sidewalk. You're my date and a reflection of me and my taste. Now shave and get dressed." She turned to leave, then stopped. "You know how to tie a tie don't you?"

"Yes, Maria, I think I can manage it."

"Good. I'll meet you in the lobby in ten minutes."

She left, but even after the door clicked shut I could feel her presence in the room.

My final inspection took place in the lobby. First, she removed a bit of lint from my jacket. Then she straightened my tie. "My boss arrived a few minutes ago. They're waiting." She pointed to the front door where we could see a large black limousine. Arm in arm, we walked together into the warm and eventful night.

***

"*Buenas Noches, Miguel,*" Maria said to the driver, "*Que pasa?*"

"*Buenas noches, senora. Todos estan bien.*"

Once we were settled Maria introduced me to our companions for the evening. Our host, Don Ricardo Juarez, came first. He was Maria's boss and a fellow Puerto Rican. Sporting at least fifty extra pounds, the man had a high forehead and a gray goatee. Everyone, including his son, referred to him as *Don Ricardo* or *El Jefe.*

His companion, a woman less than half his age, sat next to him. She wore a silver sequined dress and lots of jewelry. I never learned her name.

Next, I met Marcos, Don Ricardo's son and heir. He spoke perfect English, the result of his childhood in New York. He didn't have a female companion.

There were two other men in the limo, one named Luis, the other Guillermo, both dressed in dark suits. When one of them leaned over, I noticed a gun in his shoulder holster.

We drank as we rode. My glass had magical properties. No matter how much I drank, it never emptied. Lively salsa music played through the speakers, maintained the jolly mood.

"Don Ricardo planned this dinner several weeks ago in honor of our clients, Señor Guzman and his wife. They're from Panama,"

Maria explained. "They're in the US hoping to invest in real estate in the Washington area."

I smiled and said little as Maria chatted with Marcos and Don Ricardo in Spanish. I cursed myself for not paying closer attention in my ninth grade Spanish class.

The limo stopped in front of a restaurant named *Carne* in Georgetown. The head waiter came out to greet us and directed us to a large round table where the Guzman's were waiting.

Señora Guzman spoke no English. The husband had command of only a few words. The Señora had a ring on each finger. She wore an expensive dress over her ample figure. El Señor wore an Armani suit.

The festivities started with shots of tequila and continued with wine. It ended, much later, with tiny glasses of liqueur. Between the beginning of the dinner and its end, we ate meat, lots of meat. Waiters came to the table with loaded skewers and carved off portions onto our plates with large knives.

At one point, Maria excused herself, and I announced that I also needed to use *el bano*. In the hallway, I asked her, "Why are they so nice to me?"

"Why not? You're my friend, and they find you interesting."

I found the second part strange. I had hardly said anything. As I made my way back to the table, I saw Marcos in the lobby talking with a man in a rumpled suit. The man bore a striking resemblance to man I hit with a hammer in the rain in New Jersey. *Was he a cousin, a brother?* I continued to stare until Maria emerged from the ladies room and led me back to the table.

After we had sat down, Don Ricardo turned to me and said, "Maria tells me that you are a pilot."

"Yes, and I own my own airplane." Ricardo seemed impressed.

"Your airplane, how many kilos can it carry?"

That stopped me in mid-swallow. The table grew silent as they waited for my answer. Maria poked my side. I took a breath.

"It can carry me and 300 pounds."

Ricardo needed no calculator. "About one hundred thirty-six kilos. How fast can it go?"

"It's not fast. It travels at about 110 miles per hour. It's much faster to take a commercial flight most of the time." I began to sweat.

"Yes, but when I fly on a commercial flight, I have to wait in line and take off my shoes. If I fly with you, can I keep my shoes?" he asked with a chuckle.

Don Ricardo's mirth signaled everyone else to laugh. I laughed too as I thought of the portly man in the passenger seat of my plane with or without his shoes.

"Yes, Don Ricardo, you may keep your shoes on. I would be honored to fly you to your destinations," I responded with as much grace as I could muster.

My hypothetical passenger nodded, and the conversation changed to other topics. Ricardo focused on his son and the news that Marcos brought from the lobby. It must have been bad news. Both men seemed worried.

"Maria, is something wrong? Did I say something to upset Don Ricardo?" *Maybe the men the men in New Jersey were somehow connected to El Jefe.* But Maria ignored my questions. She had joined a conversation with the Guzmans in Spanish.

Finally, as if a cloud had passed through the room, the mood brightened again. Don Ricardo told a joke in Spanish, and Maria leaned over to translate. Her hand rested on my shoulder, her mouth whispered just inches from my ear. I did my best to maintain my composure.

Finally, we raised our glasses one more time, and Don Ricardo intoned: *"Salud, dinero, amor y el tiempo para disfrutarlos!"*

Maria translated: "Health, money, love, and the time to enjoy them."

***

I fell asleep on Maria's shoulder as soon as we entered the limo and didn't wake up until we were in front of the hotel. Maria walked me to my room, and when I fumbled with my key card, she took it and led me into my own room.

As soon as I took off my jacket, my stomach signaled an emergency. I fell to my knees and delivered half-digested meat, champagne, wine, and tequila into the toilet. I flushed, stood up, and then fell to my knees for a second round. Maria joined me. She sat on the side of the tub and rubbed my back while I leaned over the bowl.

"*Pobrecito*, you drank too much, you ate too quickly, and you are very tired."

She had removed her jewelry, shoes, and jacket. The wet washcloth she handed me was nice. I washed my face and then continued to make more contributions to the Washington Metro sewage system.

Maria left me to my misery and went to the sink and carefully washed her face. Then she took off her blouse. She inspected it closely. I guess it didn't pass muster because she put it in the sink and washed it using the hotel's hand soap. She rinsed it twice, wrung it out and hung on a towel rack.

I knelt on the floor during her ablutions. I stared unbelievingly at the half-dressed woman, wearing nothing but her bra from the waist up, whom I had met only two nights before. Maria must have seen my stare but ignored it.

When she finished with her blouse, Maria reached both thumbs under her skirt and pulled down her panties. The garment went into the sink where it received the same treatment afforded to the blouse.

The bra came next. Was this a strip tease? No. When she reached behind her back to unfasten her bra clasp, she did it the same way I had seen my wife do it a thousand times. Her breasts fell out for my inspection in the harsh bathroom light.

Maria's concentration focused on the garment she just removed, I enjoyed looking at her two newly revealed orbs. They were bigger than my wife's but not grossly enormous. There was a brown birth mark on her left breast, the one nearest to me, a fault that just made her more real, more captivating. "Maria, you're beautiful," I said from my position on the floor.

"Finish what you're doing and take a shower. It's late," she replied. The bra must have been adequately clean because she took it with her, un-washed, as she left the bathroom. We could have been married for decades.

About twenty minutes later my stomach spasms ceased. Emotionally and physically exhausted I showered and then turned to the bathroom door holding my rumpled clothes in my hand. *What would I find on the other side? Did Maria return to her room? Is she in bed? Will she want sex?* I had no idea.

The night light in the bathroom reflected off of Maria's jewelry and clothing neatly arranged on the desk and desk chair. I could see her shoes lined up at the foot of the bed as if they belonged there. I stood naked in the semi-dark not knowing what to do until Maria ordered, "Come to bed."

I did. As I got under the covers, she turned and kissed me on the cheek saying "Sweet dreams" That startled me since those were the same words I said to my daughters each night.

She turned her back to me and fell asleep. Soon her rhythmic breathing lulled me to sleep as well.

***

My bladder demanded attention a few hours later. Returning from the bathroom, I realized, once again, that a naked woman shared in my bed — and the woman was definitely not my wife.

My lust, a persistent, ember during the previous two days, erupted into a flame. I slipped under the covers and touched her shoulder. She turned, and without a word, covered my mouth with hers. We kissed for the first time — the kiss seemed to last forever. The tongue that fascinated me at lunch invaded my mouth and entwined with mine. We kicked off the covers. Our hands explored each other's bodies.

Minutes later, she climbed on top of me and effortlessly our bodies conjoined. Connected, we moved together faster and faster. I wanted to last, to satisfy her, but the sensations were too much. My dam burst. Her smile, as she looked down on me, reminded me of the smile on angles in Renaissance paintings. Her breasts and her hair dangled in my face, just as I had imagined in my dream the first night we met.

Except for grunts and sighs, neither of us had said a word.

"*Ay Chico!* What are we going to do with you?" she said as she rolled off. Apparently, "*Chico*" was to be my bedroom name.

She lay in the crook of my arm as my breathing returned to normal. Then she took my hand and showed me how to pleasure her. "With your hands, *Chico,* with your fingers!"-

"*Más alto, más abajo* my lover, commanded in Spanish as her passion increased. I did my best to accede by moving my fingers higher or lower. Her face began to get red. Her legs began to quiver. "Now *con la lengua,*" and just in case I didn't understand the noun she grabbed my hair as she pushed my mouth into her crotch. She screamed something in Spanish and grabbed a pillow to cover her face and then screamed again. A flood of female juices covered my face. I tried to pull away, but she grabbed my head and returned it to its assigned position. Then her whole body quivered again and then again.

"Enough," she said and let me come up for air.

The room smelled funky. Her side of the bed was soaking wet.

I didn't know what to do or say. *Okay, it happened, but now it has to stop. How do I ask her to get dressed and return to her own room?* But I didn't ask her to leave. I just lay on my back and said, "Wow."

She laughed and said, "Wow indeed."

We showered together. First, I stood behind her and rubbed the soap over her breasts. Her nipples hardened delightfully under my fingers. "I must have the cleanest breasts in Washington," she said.

We switched positions. I faced the wall, as she washed my back and stroked my penis. Then one of her fingers, lubricated with soap and warm water, found its way into my behind. Her left hand strummed my front while her right hand provided a counterpoint against my prostate. I became a musical instrument, and she became the maestro. I leaned against the wall and tried to remember to breathe.

The crescendo occurred when her head found its way under my left arm. I thought she was coming up for a kiss. Instead, her teeth grabbed my left nipple and bit it hard. The shot of pain got confused with the pleasurable sensations from my front and rear. Combined, they unleashed two tsunamis. One started in my toes and traveled upwards while the other started in my head and traveled down. Closer and closer they came and then, finally, crashed together in my center. Then the waves parted for an instant and crashed together again.

Unable to stand, I collapsed in the tub, surrendering to the colossus standing over me. From my position, I saw her oak-like legs, her bulging vulva and then, further upward, her breasts like two horizontal hills. Maria's face looked down from somewhere in the stratosphere — a glowing face framed with very wet, very

black hair. She laughed. I smiled. I didn't have th\
laugh.

"Did you like that *Chico*?" she said.

I didn't have the words or the strength to respon\
we were done for the night. Then, Maria squatted s\
used her hands to spread her lower lips bringing her op\
just inches above my face. "Look at me *Chico*, look a\

I looked. For a moment nothing else happened. We\
in place. My entire field of vision was absorbed by l\
hood. Then, without a word of warning, she release\
urine in my face.

"You're mine, *Chico*. With this I mark you."

Chapter 10

What now?

The bathtub wasn't designed for two adults. Maria left, taking the hair dryer with her. I stayed to wash my face and hair thoroughly before wrapping a towel around my middle, and re-entering the bedroom.

I found Maria, naked, drying her hair. Her full breasts swayed back and forth as she moved the dryer from hand to hand. Her nipples, bright pink in contrast to her brown skin, seemed to wink at me from their reflection in the dresser mirror. Once again, Maria ignored my stare.

"I'm going to spend the rest of the night in my room so you can get some sleep," she said. She walked over to the desk and stepped into her skirt. "I know you need to work tomorrow."

I turned my back to her as I pulled on the boxer shorts I normally wear while sleeping. "Maria, you know that I'm married, don't you?"

"Ay, *Chico*, of course, I know you're married. You told me you were married when we first met. Someday you will tell me all about your wife and how much you love her."

She secured the zipper on the side of her skirt and continued. "But tonight was not about your wife. It was about you and me — two humans who found each other in a hotel room at a moment when we needed each other." She donned her suit jacket directly over her naked breasts.

"I like you, Dan," she continued, "but tonight wasn't about love. We needed to be together. That's all."

I sat on the bed mesmerized by this reverse striptease. "Will I see you at breakfast? Do you need a ride to work today?"

Maria could switch from sentimentality to practical matters in a heartbeat. There were so many questions rolling around in my head. The first and most important: *Will we do it again?*

"Yes, let's meet for breakfast. No, I don't need a ride."

"Great, 7:30?" I made a move to hug her, but she turned away. "Not now, Dan, I'll see you later." She blew me a kiss and was gone.

I set up a 7:00 a.m. wake-up call and tried to go back to sleep. The sheets still held her smell. Her last words in the bathroom still echoed in my mind. "You are mine. With this I mark you."

It was scary and exciting at the same time. It was exciting because it was scary. The sheets were a poor substitute Maria, but they were soft against my hardness. They were sufficient. The heat flowed from my head to my groin. At first, I fought against the impulse but finally surrendered to oblivion for the third time that night.

***

I awoke on Thursday feeling spent, guilty and giddy all at the same time. My back hurt from the bathtub experience. There was an unfamiliar tenderness in my groin.

Was I unfaithful? I didn't want to confront the question. On the one hand, I did have sex with another woman. On the other hand, it was not as if I planned it. It just happened. It was her fault.

I knew that the argument was bullshit. Of course, I was unfaithful. I put the issue into a compartment at the back of my mind for later examination.

I made a cup of weak hotel-room-coffee and retrieved my

voice mail messages. There were three, all from Beth. In the first one, she sounded annoyed. The second sounded more annoyed. By the third message, she had reached new heights of annoyedness. And she had a good reason for her attitude. I hadn't been communicating with her during her very trying time.

Beth picked up on the first ring.

"Well, it is about time. Where the hell have you been? Where are you anyway?"

"Beth, I told you. I'm in Rockville. I had to attend a working dinner with a prospective new client. I didn't get back until late. I sent you a text. I didn't want to ..."

"You didn't have time for a phone call? Your daughter's in the hospital, and you all you could do is to send me a bullshit text?"

I gulped. "You're right. I should have called. How are you?"

"Fuck you. If you cared about me, you would have called yesterday."

There was silence.

"Beth, are you there?"

"Yes, I'm here. I just walked outside to get some air."

"How's Amy?"

"Amy will be in the hospital until tomorrow. They have her zonked out on pain meds. I'm exhausted. I slept in a chair beside her bed last night. I've been drinking too much coffee and eating too much crap food in the hospital cafeteria."

"How's Sara?"

"She's okay, I guess. She stayed at a friend's house last night. She keeps nagging me about the cell phone and ..."

Silence again.

"Are you there?"

"Yes, God damn it. I'm here. I just found a bench to sit on. My hair's a mess. I need a shower. When are you coming home?"

"I'll be home Friday. I'll try to leave early. Go buy Sara her cell phone. We have the money. I got an advance from my new client and ..."

"I thought you said that it was a prospective client?"

"Yes, well I guess it's for real. We're still working out the details, but they gave me a substantial retainer. I deposited $5,000 into our account yesterday."

"Well hallelujah. What about the plane? Did you sell the plane?"

"No, I ... "

"Did you at least place the ad like you promised?"

"Not yet. I may need the plane as part of this contract and ... "

"God Damn it, Dan. You promised!"

"Yes, I know but this new contract ... "

"Dan, I don't have time for your bullshit. You're lying about something."

"Beth, I'm ... "

"Save it. I'm going. Bye."

I said "Goodbye" to a disconnected cell phone.

***

Maria wasn't there when I got to the restaurant. Thankful for a few minutes alone, I scanned the local pages of the *Washington Post* for the story I dreaded finding. It was on page three, in the local section. The headline read, "One Dead on Northern Beltway." The rest of the article was taken from the police report. A car went out of control and smashed into the guardrail, causing a chain reaction of fender benders. The driver of the car that caused the accident was found dead at the scene. His identity was withheld pending notification of family members.

I could feel the sweat breaking out on my forehead. *Was it Richard? It was certainly his car. Maybe it was stolen? Maybe he loaned it to a friend?*

You're grasping at straws. Of course, it was Richard. The

chain of events was obvious. Richard left the hotel, drove on the Beltway, lost control and died from blood loss. What do I do with the cocaine?

Richard had my business card. Did he have it on him when he died? His blood was all over my airplane. Should I contact his sister? My breath came in short gasps.

Maria arrived.-"Good morning, Dan." Her voice was bright and, overly loud. Several diners looked in our direction. I was certain that the men were jealous. I moved my left hand under the table to hide my wedding ring.

Maria, oblivious to the reaction, sat down and added the word "again" softly. She wore dark slacks and a gray sweater that seemed a size too small. When she moved in a certain way, I could see her nipples poking against the fabric. Her familiar gold cross rested in the valley between the two mounds. Was the religious symbol a warning sign — a sort of "X," warning me to keep away — or was it an arrow pointing downward to the delightful places that I explored just a few hours ago?

We just smiled at each other. I said "good morning" in a nonchalant way. Maria ordered her food. I drank my second cup of coffee and continued to scan the newspaper. Finally, I gathered my courage and spoke. "Maria, are you free tonight? Do you want to see me?" I was as shy as a teenager asking for a prom date. She smiled and touched my wrist.

"You're such a child, *Chico*," she said in a whisper. "Is this the first time you have been with another woman since you were married?"

I nodded.

"Yes, I am free. Tonight you will take me to dinner — somewhere very romantic. Before we meet, you will call your wife and take care of all of your business. We will have a lovely dinner and then return to my room. You will be with me, and I will be with you, and we will forget about everything and everyone else."

***

A half hour later, I nervously walked to my rental car wondering if I would find it vandalized with the trunk ripped open. Instead, it sat undisturbed in its assigned place. As casually as possible, I opened the trunk. The duffle bag of narcotics stared back at me like a kidnap victim.

I decided that if the bag were still there when I finished teaching that day, it would be a sign from God that I was doing the right thing. God and I didn't talk together on a regular basis. I was quite willing to assume that He or She either didn't exist or was too occupied with other events in the universe to hear my pleas. That day was different. I was dealing with things I wasn't used to dealing with. I was flying blind and looking to a higher power for guidance.

Maria gave me a set of orders. I was looking to God for a second opinion.

***

"Hi Dan, do you want me to teach today?" Michelle asked as I entered the classroom.

"How about I teach the morning, and you teach the afternoon?" I replied. "I need to leave early to visit a potential client."

"That's fine. Here is where we stopped yesterday."

"You got that far? You must be very good."

She smiled and said, "I've learned from the master."

I had a hard time at first. But after the first half an hour, I found my rhythm and the class went reasonably well. I was gratified to see Michelle taking notes.

She came to my desk as the class broke for lunch. "That was great. I liked the way you used humor to make your points. I need to do that more often. Would you like to have lunch together?"

We took the elevator to the basement cafeteria, a huge windowless room with food and drink stations at one end. Michelle went to the salad bar. I opted for lasagna. After paying, I found Michelle waving at me from a far corner. She was sitting at a table with two strangers.

"Dan I want you to meet my friends Mike Henderson and Phil Swanson. They both work in the building. Mike, Phil, this is Dr. Dan Goldberg."

"Call me Dan, please," I said extending my hand.

Michelle continued the conversation. "Dan wrote a textbook on applied statistics. He has been teaching here for the past six months."

I looked at the two men. One word described the both of them — large. They were over six feet tall with very broad shoulders. Mike sported a blond crew cut. Phil was bald. They were both wearing sports coats, which I thought was unusual. The cafeteria was hot. Summer was only two days away. Everyone else, including me, wore only the bare minimum.

As I started to eat, I asked, "What do you guys do? Do you also work with the FDA?"

Mike responded, "No, we're with the Drug Enforcement Administration, the DEA. We investigate narcotics trafficking." He said this matter-of-factly as he used his fork to twirl spaghetti on his plate.

Oh, my God, I'm having lunch with men assigned to investigate me.

"Dan, are you ok?" Michelle said, "You're not breathing."

I gulped some water. "I'm fine. That sounds like exciting work."

"Not really, for the most part, we sit behind desks and analyze data."

"What kind of data?"

"We analyze all kinds of data," Phil replied. "Right now we're looking at data from the FAA concerning flights of private aircraft. We've been trying to correlate them with reports of drug deals, murders, stolen vehicles, etc. It's tough going."

Michelle, trying to be helpful, chimed in. "You know, Dan is great at analyzing data. Maybe he could help?"

Michelle, please keep your mouth shut. I don't need a job proving I'm guilty.

Mike's eyes brightened. "Do you have a card? We might be able to use your expertise from time to time. There's so much data. We have trouble keeping up."

I handed a card to each of them with a shaking hand and, in exchange, received theirs. I couldn't eat. The remaining lasagna suddenly smelled like manure. I'm sure it showed on my face.

"Dan, are you sick?" Michelle asked, "Is there something wrong with the food?"

"You know, there might be. I don't feel well. I might be allergic to something. I'm going to leave now. Michelle, can you teach the rest of the class?"

"Don't worry. I think I can handle it. Go back to your hotel and rest."

I rose holding my tray. "Thanks, Michelle. I'll see you in the morning. It was nice meeting you, Mike and Phil." The two just stared at me, and I was sure that they were trying to memorize my face.

I stopped in the men's room and washed my face. I made a mental list of all the things that could be used to trace the murders back to me. The most damaging item was Richard's blood all over the inside of my plane. Like Macbeth's wife, I needed to erase the blood as soon as possible.

Approaching my rental car in the parking structure, I was certain that someone was watching. I didn't open the trunk. As casually as possible, I got into the car and drove out of the parking garage keeping one eye on my rear view mirror.

Chapter 11

Into Hot Water

On the way back to the hotel, I stopped at a McDonalds for a quick lunch. There, I watched a two-year-old climb up and down the indoor playground as his parents applauded his accomplishments.

Beth and I felt the same way when our first daughter was born. I was a graduate student then. We lived in a one-bedroom apartment decorated with yard sale furniture and books. Compared to our current lifestyle, we had nothing. Yet we were happy. Every smile and gurgle that came out of Sara's mouth were gifts from God. When did we lose that feeling? Why was I risking arrest just to get more money to get more stuff? And when did I get so horny?

A part of my mind could rationalize that first night with Maria. I was drunk. But now, completely sober, how could I justify a second date with the lady?

I put the unanswered question in a deep, dark part at the back of my mind. Maybe some questions are better left unanswered?

With Maria out of the way, my mind wandered to the duffle full of cocaine. Maybe I should just take the dope to the nearest police station and confess? I'd return to my family, sell the plane, and look for a job. But will I be able to lie well enough to turn in the drugs and keep the cash?

I tried to imagine interrogation. I'm in a windowless room.

There's a one-way mirror on the wall. A metal table and two chairs, all bolted to the floor, are the only furniture. Two detectives enter. One is black. One is white. The white cop hands me a Styrofoam cup of weak coffee.

"Okay Goldberg why don't you tell us how you got money and dope. And don't leave out the part about that hot piece of ass you been playing with."

Most of the dialog came from watching *Law and Order* episodes. But the daydream made it clear that if I went to the police, Maria would be brought in making it impossible to hide the affair from my wife.

Which way to turn? That's when I looked through the window and saw a young black man standing on the street corner not far from the restaurant. A late model car pulled up to him. The young man leaned into the window. Then he sauntered around the corner while the men in the car waited. After a few minutes, the young man returned and handed something to the people in the car.

I had just watched a drug deal. By simply sitting in an almost empty McDonalds, I was getting a lesson in retail drug dealing.

Minutes later another car pulled up, and the scene replayed. Could I do that? I tried to imagine myself standing on the corner wearing torn jeans, music plugged into my ears.

It wouldn't work. For one thing, I couldn't find a way to combine light rock with street-side drug deals. Nor did I have the courage to approach the young man, contact his boss and try to sell the drugs wholesale. That's when I resolved, once again, to dump the bag out of my plane into the Chesapeake Bay. That will be the end of it.

On the way back to the hotel I assuaged my guilt by transferring another eight thousand dollars into the Goldberg joint account. Then, feeling like I had matters firmly in hand, I stripped, collapsed on the bed and tried to take a nap.

***

My cell phone sounded its distinctive ring.

"Yeah?"

"That's no way to answer a phone." It was my wife.

"What time is it?"

"It's five thirty in the afternoon. Were you sleeping?"

"Trying to. I ate something funny at lunch and let the new instructor finish the class. I came back to the hotel for a nap." I looked longingly at the sheets, knowing that my plan was toast.

"New instructor?"

"Yeah, they hired a new woman. I let her sit in on the class. How's Amy?"

"Aside from a bad attitude, she's ok. The doc gave her more pain pills. They've knocked her out. Hey, I just checked our bank balance. Where did all that money come from?"

"I think I told you. I landed a new contract."

"They paid in advance? What do they do?"

"Something to do with real estate. I'll learn more later on. How've you been?"

"I'm exhausted. On top of everything else, my car stalled twice today."

"I'm not surprised. It's a piece of junk. Why don't you start shopping for a new one?"

"We can't afford it."

"I think we can. This new contract — "

"You've said that before — "

"It will work this time. And, it's a long-term contract."

"We'll see. Did you place an ad to sell the plane?"

"No — "

"You promised."

"I know, but things have changed and — "

"*Things* haven't changed. *You've* changed."

There was a pause. I held my breath expecting Beth to continue with "sell the plane or else." That could be my justification for continuing the relationship with Maria. But she just left the thought unfinished.

"I need to keep the airplane," I said, "so I can meet with the owner at a moment's notice."

"Bullshit! Liar!"

"I'm not — "

"I need to go."

She didn't hang up. We could hear each other breathing in the silence. It wasn't just any silence to me. It was Beth's special way of being silent. It was my wife's silence that I've grown to love over the years.

Her breath brought back memories of those hot Jamaican nights during our honeymoon. Translating thoughts into action, my hand slipped into my briefs. "Where are you right now?" I asked.

"I'm in the kitchen, putting the lunch dishes away. Dan, I need to go."

"What are you wearing?"

"I was gardening. I'm still wearing dirty denim shorts and a t-shirt. I'm sure I smell like a horse." Then in a hushed voice, "What are you doing? Are you touching yourself?"

"I'm lying on the bed thinking about our honeymoon. Do you remember those nights and all that dope we smoked?"

"Hold on." After a few seconds, she continued, "I'm in the downstairs bathroom so the girls can't hear me. Yes, I remember Jamaica. I was so sore, I could hardly sit for a week. That's where we made Sara. Are you naked?"

"Yes and I'm … "

Through the phone, I could hear my daughter's voice. "Mom I need to use the bathroom."

"I need to go. Keep thinking about me." Then, with a chuckle, she added, "Pervert."

I watched the late afternoon shadows climb the wall while my passion ebbed.

The nap wasn't going to happen, so I headed for the pool and started doing laps. After three laps I lost myself into the chlorine-scented present.

Six later, a woman started doing laps in the lane furthest from mine. Somehow we were always at opposite ends of the pool. Curious, I sat on the edge and waited. Sure enough, it was Maria now attired in a black, one-piece Speedo swimsuit. She wore a white swim cap.

She saw me swam over. "Hi Dan, where are we eating?" She took off the swim cap to shake out her raven hair. I wasn't looking at her hair. The cold water created twin bumps that seemed to wink at me through the tight Spandex.

"It'll be a surprise. We need to be there at 7:30. It's close, we can walk there."

"Let's go soak in the hot tub."

The delightfully hot water and noisy jets discouraged conversation. Neither of us had much to say anyway. We lay back and surrendered to the bubbles.

After a few minutes, a woman in her early twenties entered. Maria waved her over. "That's my friend Esmeralda," Maria said as she left the tub. The women conversed in rapid-fire Spanish.

They were a study in contrasts: Maria was a head taller and at least 50 pounds heavier than her friend. Whatever extra pounds she carried, just emphasized her luscious curves. Esmeralda was skinny. Her hip bones showed above her bikini bottoms while her breasts didn't quite fill her top.

It was clear to me that the women were more than passing acquaintances. They touched each other as they spoke. Finally, they hugged and parted. Esmeralda started swimming laps.

"How do you know Esmeralda?" I asked.

"We worked together in the New York office." Maria lowered

herself into the hot swirling water and came to my side. "I'm sorry I didn't include you in the conversation."

"What's she doing in the Washington area?"

"She's entertaining a client. It's just a coincidence that we're both in the same hotel at the same time."

I watched Esmeralda swim back and forth with smooth, athletic strokes. Maria noticed me watching her friend and asked, "So, *Chico* am I not enough for you? Do you like the skinny women with flat chests?" *Was she jealous or just teasing me?*

"No Maria, I like your breasts just the way they are."

I closed my eyes luxuriating on the warm water. Seated about four feet from Maria we were just two hotel guests who happened to be using the hot tub at the same time. If my wife walked into the pool area, I would have nothing to be embarrassed about. *"Oh, Hi Beth, I'd like to introduce you to this nice person I recently met."* I pictured Beth entering the pool area. She would be wearing her faded blue bathing suit. The two women would shake hands and —

A big toe massaged the front of my swim trunks. The toe belonged to my smiling girlfriend. She flexed her foot again.

"I can tell that you were thinking about a woman *Chico*. Who was it? Was it Esmeralda?"

I blushed and moved away. "Come on, Maria. I already said that you are more than I can handle."

"You're lying. Men want to fuck anything they can get their hands on." Maria glided next to me and started massaging my thigh with her strong hands. "Yes, *Chico* you can look at Esmeralda. Look at her small, tight ass. It's like a boy's. Are you into boy-like asses?" I didn't answer. We kissed, and she guided my hand inside the bottom of her swimsuit. She gasped and bit my lip as my thumb found a special spot.

Her hand was in my trunks. "Ay, *Chico*. What are we going to do with you?" Answering her own question she commanded,

"Come with me."

I grabbed a towel to hide the bulge in my trunks and followed Maria to the small sauna room at the other end of the room. *Strange, she seems to know all the secret places. Has she done this before?*

The door closed. Our mouths entwined. It wasn't a kiss. It was some kind of urgent and needful union. Without disengaging, she struggled out of the top part of her wet swimsuit.

We broke apart, breathing heavily, staring into each other's eyes. Her right hand came out of nowhere and slapped my face. "Now, *Chico*," she demanded and turned to face the back wall while pulling her swimsuit down to her knees. She grabbed the bench and arched her back towards me — an unmistakable invitation.

We quickly became one sweaty, slimy, chlorine-smelling organism. Our minds disengaged and our bodies started to move in a now familiar rhythm. The cedar bench provided a creaking accompaniment to our sensual dance. We contributed a chorus of guttural moans. Unable to restrain myself, I released ten thousand little Goldbergs into Maria's welcoming slit.

She pushed me away and tried to turn around, but the Speedo prevented a graceful maneuver. She ended up on the floor, her legs waving in the air.

"Oh my God, Maria, you're going to get us kicked out."

She just laughed.

***

We returned to our separate rooms to get dressed for dinner. I checked the TV news for any more information about the accident on the Beltway. Then I heard a knock on the door.

I panicked, looking around the room for incriminating evidence. After the third knock, I looked through the peephole. It was Maria.

"Hi, I thought I'd pick you up," she said.

"Great, I'm ready," I said holding her waist and kissing her on the cheek. I wasn't comfortable kissing her on the lips when we weren't in the midst of passion.

Instead of heading for the door, Maria took a small mirror and a familiar glassine envelope from her purse. She sprinkled the powder and asked me for a bill. She rolled it into a tube and expertly snorted a line. She handed the tube to me with a quizzical look.

"Maria, is that cocaine?"

"Yes, you've tried it?"

"Once, long ago," I lied.

"Just sniff," she said handing me the tube. "Sniff like you're smelling a flower."

That startled me, and I remembered my first encounter with the drug while trapped in Richard's car. Did Maria know Richard? Did they purchase the drug from the same cocaine emporium?

I refused. She shrugged and made the second line disappear. When Beth and I visited friends, we would bring a bottle of wine. Our social circle knew nothing about cocaine. In Maria's world, cocaine was as popular as Chardonnay.

"Come here *Chico*," she said from the desk chair. When I got close enough, she grabbed my belt, opened my pants, pulled my underwear to my knees and started sucking.

I really didn't want to have sex again. My emotions were confused. On the one hand, I felt guilty. On the other hand, I was excited and proud of the fact that I had seduced this wanton creature.

It was somewhat similar to the feelings I had when I was ten years old. It was the end of summer, just a week before the start of school. For months, I was anticipating our annual trip to the state fair. I was finally tall enough to go on the "Monster" roller coaster, but my mother said, "No, it will make you sick, wait till next year." A year in the life of a ten-year-old is an eternity.

I had money saved up from my chores and was determined to go anyway. After we had parked, Mom asked me to empty my pockets. I had ten dollars. "That's too much." She took all but one dollar saying, "Find me, and I'll give you more."

But, I had a plan. After we had parted, I extracted two more dollars from my shoe then ran to the coaster and stood proudly in front of the plywood sign saying, "you must be this high."

"OK kid, you can go," the man said. "That's a buck a ticket." I handed him a sweat-soaked bill. He looked at it suspiciously and admitted me through the gate. The ride went up and down and twisted in every way. At the top of each cycle, I was weightless for a fraction of a second. That continued for three or four minutes. When it stopped, I went behind a tent and threw up. Mom was right — I did get sick. But I was right —the ride was great. I was flying for an instant in a sheet metal imitation of an airplane. Most importantly, I got away with it and realized that I always had to have a plan.

So there I was in the hotel room, my pants at my knees, Maria using her mouth to excite me. I had no plan. The animal part of my brain took over, and despite my efforts to the contrary, I exploded into Maria's throat.

Maria made her way to the bathroom. After a short time, she emerged neat and presentable. With one exception: Her eyes were dilated, and she had a weird smile on her face.

"Come *Chico*. We'll be late for dinner."

Chapter 12

Dinner Date

We left the hotel a few minutes before seven. "Let's walk," I said. "It's only six blocks."

"In this heat? No way, let's take my car."

"We're walking. I need the exercise."

"Just wait till after dinner. I'll give you exercise." She slid her purse strap over her head and took my hand. "You're the one who'll get hot wearing that jacket."

"I know, but the restaurant requires a jacket for men."

Maria led the way with a jaunty step. That night she wore a short, black pleated skirt and a white sleeveless top held in place by a neat bow behind her neck. She had piled her hair on top of her head in a French braid.

I followed a few steps behind. *What am I doing?* I could rationalize the previous night's sexual gymnastics as a kind of accident. I was drunk. She took advantage of me. It was as if I stepped off the curb and twisted my ankle. If I canceled the date that night, I could confess everything to Beth. After all, accidents happen.

How could I explain the encounter in the sauna, a few hours ago? That was wrong, no two ways about it. That would have to stay a secret.

So what are you doing now? You know what'll happen when you return to the hotel. This is it. We'll go to dinner and then say good night, and I'll never see her again.

She waited at the street corner for me to catch up. "Hurry up slowpoke. We just missed the light. What are you thinking about?"

"I was just thinking about my daughter and her broken arm. That's all. The restaurant's on the next block."

A big articulated bus roared by close the curb creating a momentary whirlwind. Maria's skirt flew skyward exposing the lower half of her body.

In the seconds it took for gravity to restore her modesty, brakes screeched, a horn honked, and a weary office worker showed his appreciation with a wolf whistle. I couldn't blame him. Her black panties looked great against her brown skin. Lit by passing head-lights, Maria put the famous Marilyn Monroe pose to shame.

Maria laughed as she adjusted her skirt. "Did you like that *Chico?*"

I gulped down the saliva in my mouth and nodded my head in agreement. I did like it. I could feel my earlier resolve start to erode like the snow in an April rain.

***

Alfredo's was a "couples only" restaurant. Each table was nestled in a high-walled, three-sided alcove. Heavy curtains flanked the remaining side. A quick pull on the two velvet ropes would lower the curtains creating a private room.

We decided on the chef's fixed price menu and ordered a bottle of white wine to go with our first course. Maria insisted on oysters. "You need to eat oysters, *Chico.* They'll give you strength for what I've planned tonight." The food, wine, soft music (Smokey Robinson), and dim lighting created a very romantic mood. We sat close together, Maria's hand resting on my thigh.

Just as I sucked up the juice of the last mollusk, Esmeralda passed our booth. Her companion was Senor Guzman, the guest of honor at Don Ricardo's dinner the night before. Esmeralda wore a short white summer dress. As they passed, Maria smiled and waved. Esmeralda waved back and blew Maria a kiss. They settled into the next booth.

"The Señor isn't with his wife tonight," I said with a smirk. Somehow, seeing another man having dinner with a woman, not his wife provided a kind of justification for my actions.

"No, he isn't," Maria replied. "I'm sure he told his wife that he had a boring business dinner. Don Ricardo doesn't want his wealthy clients to miss any excitement while they're in the U.S." She took a sip of wine. "Esmeralda is one of our best."

"So she's a … " I couldn't find the word. Suddenly the low lights, the semi-private alcove, the red wallpaper, began to feel tawdry rather than risqué and romantic. I could feel beads of sweat running down my back. I moved a few inches away from Maria as the appetizer was replaced by our salads.

Five minutes passed in silence. If Esmeralda's profession was what I thought it was, and if she and Maria worked together, what does that make Maria? And what does that make our relationship? Finally, Maria broke the silence with one word — "Hostess."

"You want me to get the hostess?" I asked.

Maybe we can cut the dinner short, and I can get some sleep tonight.

"No, *estúpido,* the word you couldn't get out of your big gringo mouth was 'hostess.' Esmeralda is a hostess. Her assignment this week is to accompany Senor Guzman when he isn't with his wife. She is his translator and companion."

Maria finished the wine in her glass then refilled it from the bottle. I drank water.

What did I get myself into? Why did I tell her about my wife and daughters?

It was my turn to talk. I didn't want to explore the deeper meaning of the word "hostess." Instead, I asked, "How did you come to work for Don Ricardo?"

"Someday *Chico*, I may answer your question. Both the one you asked and the one you are afraid to ask. Instead, I will tell you a little about my life before I met Don Ricardo."

That seemed to relieve the mood. I finished the wine in the bottle and signaled for a bottle of Burgundy.

"I was born in the village of Carolina on the Southwest coast of Puerto Rico. My father owned a clothing factory, and until I was thirteen, we had a good life. I had two brothers and a sister. I was the youngest. My oldest brother, Juan, worked with my father and was destined to take over the family enterprise. Roberto, the next oldest, was studying to become a doctor. My sister Teresa was two years older than me and still in school as was I.

"We were not wildly rich, but we were very comfortable. We had servants to cook and clean. I never wanted for anything."

"That sounds wonderful," I said. "Did you have a large house with an interior courtyard?"

"Yes, and the courtyard even had a fountain." She paused,"You know I don't tell this story to just anyone." Then she smiled. "I'm starting to like you." I blushed.

"My life changed in many ways a few months after my thirteenth birthday. It was a Friday afternoon. My mother had invited some relatives for dinner and was supervising the preparations. We heard sirens, but there were often sirens in our town. Then the phone rang.

"Mama answered cheerily. I am sure she assumed that another cousin was confirming an invitation. She nodded her head and said *'Si'* several times. Then she collapsed on the floor. I screamed. The cook screamed. Roberto ran into the kitchen and called the paramedics. I kept screaming. No one paid any attention to me."

"That's horrible," I said. I could imagine what it must have been like for her. Maria paused as the waitress delivered our main course.

Maria ate a bite of meat, drank a sip of wine then said, "Mama recovered. She lay in Roberto's lap and told us that there was a fire at the factory. Many employees died in the blaze. The fire-fighters couldn't find Papa or Juan.

"Roberto went to the factory and returned to confirm the grim news. Papa, Juan and sixteen women who worked in the sewing room were dead. They couldn't get out because workers had stacked bales of cloth in front of the emergency exits."

Maria paused and wiped away a tear. She pushed her plate away. "I can't eat this."

"When did this happen?"

"It was more than twenty years ago. Sometimes it feels like yesterday. Do you want me to go on?"

"Only if you want to."

Maria nodded. "I do. I need to. Somehow I think you can understand."

"The following month was a nightmare. There were eighteen funerals. My mother wore a black dress and never left the house, not even for Papa's and Juan's funerals.

"My uncle, Julio, came from New York to take charge of the family. He negotiated with the authorities and with the insurance company. The priest wanted our family to pay for all the funerals, and provide a stipend to the worker's families but my uncle refused. Tension mounted day by day. One night, someone threw a rock through our front window. The next day Teresa came home from school with a bloody nose. We boarded a plane a few days later.

"That's how I came to New York," she concluded.

It was a long story. We finished our second bottle of wine.

"Then, sometime later you came to work for Don Ricardo?" I said.

"Don Ricardo is a distant relative through marriage." She chuckled. "I think all Puerto Ricans are related to each other somehow.

She picked at the vegetables on her plate then stared into my eyes. "What will you tell Beth about me?"

Hearing Maria vocalize my wife's name destroyed my growing empathy towards the woman. She crossed a line. She had no right to use my wife's name. Didn't she understand that these four days didn't count? They existed in some other Steven-King-like dimension. I moved away from her and started looking for the waitress. I wanted to leave.

I would say nothing to my wife. When the week was over, I would return to my wife, my family, my lawn in exactly the same way that I'd left it. That was my only plan.

Once again, we sat in silence. Finally, Maria spoke. "It's okay Dan. You're new at this. These days, these nights will be our secret. Your wife will never know." There was a practiced way she said the words. I wasn't her first married man.

Our dessert was a luscious key lime pie. As we lifted our forks, Esmeralda passed in front of our table holding her purse. The two women locked eyes and Maria said, "Uh, Dan, I need to use *el baño*." That didn't surprise me. Living with three females, I had grown used to their attachment to plumbing. Nor was I surprised when Maria's absence stretched to fifteen minutes. By then I'd finished my dessert and was surreptitiously taking small bites out of hers.

She returned with a flushed face and a mischievous glint in her eye. She pulled the curtain ropes as she entered the booth and looked at me as if I was the dessert. I felt vulnerable in the private space.

"What's going on?"

She pressed her face into my shoulder and started to giggle.

"Come on Maria, what happened in the ladies' room?" Her giggles turned into laughter. Then we heard Esmeralda's laughter coming from the booth next door.

When she recovered enough to talk she said, "I have a present for you. Open your hand." I did, and she placed something in it. I could feel a piece of fabric. "Ok, now look at it." The fabric was white and made of cotton. On closer examination, I realized I was holding a pair of woman's panties.

I was confused. Maria wore black panties. I saw them during the Marilyn Monroe-inspired whirlwind.

"Who's ... " I heard a very loud gasp from the next booth followed by Esmeralda's loud laugh. Maria pointed.

"Hers."

***

My hands were shaking as we returned to the hotel. I knew what Maria wanted. I wanted it, too, and I hated myself for the desire. A part of my mind argued. *End it now! Leave in the morning and never see her again.* All I needed to do was press the elevator button for the third floor.

Somehow Maria knew what I was thinking. She positioned herself in front of the buttons and forcefully pressed number two. Then she turned and lifted her face. "Kiss me, *Chico*. Hold me, I'm a little drunk. I tasted the wine on her tongue as she stumbled into my arms. Her smell filled my nostrils — a combination of perfume and sweat. Intoxicated, I offered no resistance as we walked to her room.

I searched for the analytical part of my brain, the part that sorted things into "right" and "wrong," but it had quit for the evening. *None of this is real, I surmised. I might as well enjoy it.*

In her typical, no-nonsense way, Maria wasted no time setting the mood. She lit an incense stick filling the room with an exotic jasmine smell. Her sandals came off and found their place at the foot of the bed. She carefully hung her skirt and blouse in the closet. Her bra went into one dresser drawer, her watch, and other jewelry into another.

"I'll be right back," she said then went into the bathroom. I could have left. I didn't. I was paralyzed — torn between what I wanted to do and what I knew I should do.

Maria re-entered the room wearing only her makeup and skimpy black panties. "*Chico*, why are you still dressed? Get naked!"

I took off my pants, shirt, shoes, and socks but retained my briefs as a faint protest against her commands. She didn't notice. Instead, she lit a joint.

It was becoming clear that Maria had a well-thought-out plan for the evening.

She turned on the TV and chose a pay-per-view movie from the adult selections. We shared the joint sitting on the bed in our underwear. The first scene featured a large woman demonstrating her masturbation technique. It concluded with a gynecological close-up along with the expected grunts and moans. The next scene had the same woman enjoying the intimate attentions of two well-endowed men.

The movie was mildly arousing. I didn't know what to do with my hands. I looked to Maria for guidance, but she showed more interest in the joint than either the movie or me.

I began to look at the movie analytically. There was a forced, clinical feel to the action. It was clear that the actors were responding to an off-camera director in each of their collisions and separations. My attention drifted away from the cast to furniture and the drapes on the movie set.

Maria noticed my flaccid condition. The evening wasn't going in the way she planned. "*Estoy aburrida,*" she said. I must have looked confused, so she translated. "I'm bored, God damit!"

She went to her dresser and hunted for something in the bottom drawer. At that moment, the actress on the screen bent over in a similar pose. The combination of the two images brought my male appendage to full attention. I discovered what I could do with my hand.

Maria noticed and smiled. Adopting the tone of a cruel mistress she scolded, "You're touching yourself, *Chico*. Who said that you can touch yourself?" She grabbed my right wrist, wrapped a rope around it, and tied the other end to the bedpost. Next, she did the same to my left. The anticipation was delightful. I had heard about couples doing this but had never experienced anything like it. *What other perversions does this woman have in store for me?*

Raking her fingernails down my chest, she grabbed my erection and squeezed. "Do you like watching, *Chico*?"

Deciding to increase the tension, Maria reached into her purse and extracted Esmeralda's undergarment. She waved it in front of my face making sure that I recognized it. "Open your mouth," she commanded. I complied, and the panties became a gag. "There professor, that will keep you quiet for a while."

I'm sure she meant to bring our eroticism to new heights. In fact, it had the opposite effect. In the restaurant, they were "panties" with all the mystery that the word contained to the ten-year-old part my brain. Now there was no mystery. I had a prostitute's dirty underwear in my mouth. I gagged and spat the filthy thing out. "Yuk! Untie me. This isn't working for me."

Maria's face collapsed in frustration. She was no longer the mistress of ropes and perversions. Her shoulders sagged. Tears formed at the corners of her eyes and her makeup began to run down her cheeks.

She covered her face with her hands and retreated to the bathroom.

With a little effort, I broke free from the ropes and got dressed. I was disgusted with myself. I needed to leave. The incense that once was romantic was now cloying.

My hand was on the doorknob when Maria emerged. She had washed her face, tied her hair back into a loose ponytail, and wore one of the hotel's white terry cloth bathrobes. "Dan, what are you doing? Where are you going?"

"Estoy aburrido," I said trying to mimic both her words and accent.

She looked at me and sighed, "Me too. Dan, please stay a little while, we need to talk."

I nodded my agreement. I owed her that much. She offered me a bottle of water from the mini-refrigerator. I sat on the bed. She sat in the desk chair facing me. I turned off TV.

"What do you want to talk about? It's late. I have to teach tomorrow." It was clear that we were at the end of our relationship. Who was leaving whom? Did it matter?

"Dan, we met because I was paid to meet you. It was part of my job."

"What …?"

"I work for Marcos. Marcos thought that you owned a fancy jet airplane. They needed someone to transport cash and drugs. I believe your friend Richard gave him the information. Marcos told me to get to know you."

Damn Richard. Even after his death, he still manages to mess up my life.

"During the dinner, Wednesday night, they learned that you weren't a hot shot pilot. You're a school teacher with a toy airplane."

"It's not a toy," I insisted.

She waved away the comment. "Dan, this is hard for me. Don't interrupt. My boss lost interest in you. I didn't. I like you. You're modest and honest. It's been a long time since I've been with a man like you. Mostly, with Don Ricardo's clients, I'm an accessory in public and a mistress in private. This week you were my boyfriend, *mi novio.*"

She rose and tried to kiss me. I turned away. "So you're a …" I couldn't finish the sentence. I couldn't look at her. *How many*

*other men had she slept with? What about the "you are mine"
crap?*

"Dan," she responded reasonably but with an edge to her
voice, "I'm a real estate agent and a translator. You might call me
an actress as well. I'm not proud of some of the things that I do,
but we all do things we're not proud of. It's the best way that I
have to take care of myself and my family."

"So you sleep with men to support your family, how noble!"
I started for the door, but Maria barred the way.

"Dan, it's not that simple. You see — "

"You're a prostitute, *una puta*." I finally found the word and
the Spanish translation. It hurt my mouth to say it.

She slapped my face then tried to punch me in the chest. I
grabbed her wrists and pushed her away.

"Fuck you, Dan! You have no idea what my life was like.
When we came to New York, after my father died, my uncle stole
all our money. Do you know what jobs are available for a Puerto
Rican woman with only a high school education? Try being a
cleaning woman. That's what my sister did. Try being a waitress
for eight hours a day and come home smelling of grease with less
than fifty dollars in your pocket. That's what I did. You walk
around, so proud of your fancy education. I had to support my
family with my guts and determination, something you never had
to do."

"Maria, I'm sorry. I'm — "

"Be careful who you're calling a whore. If I'm a whore, what
are you? You sell your mind to the highest bidder."

I tried to put my arm on her shoulder. "Get the fuck away
from me." She turned towards the window, crying.

I started for the door, still feeling the sting of her slap. "Dan
wait. Don't go yet. I do care for you. Let's part as friends."

I turned to face her. "Okay, let's be friends." She paced back
and forth. Her robe flew open with every turn showing glimpses

of her body. The view would have been sexy a dozen minutes ago. Now it was clinical. *Was that a scar on her belly? Was one breast larger than the other?*

"Maria, I need to go."

"Dan, you're an idiot. That first night when I seemed to be fascinated by your goddamn airplane I was acting." She struck a pose, shook her hair back and recalled her lines — "Oh, that's so interesting, tell me more." She paused as if waiting for applause.

I blushed. How could I have fallen for those lies?

"No applause? Oh well." She stood and looked directly into my eyes. "What happened in your hotel room last night wasn't acting. It was real."

We hugged. We cried. Finally, we broke apart. "Ok, Dan it's time to say goodbye. *Vaya con Dios.* Don't call me." She released me. I left. As the door closed I caught my last glimpse of Maria, her black hair contrasting with the white robe. I walked down the hall trying to burn that image into my memory.

Chapter 13

Home Free?

The next morning, Friday, everything seemed to go my way. The traffic moved smartly on the beltway, the security guard waved me through without searching my briefcase, even the elevator doors opened at my touch. The last day of teaching is always easy — that day was no exception. I went over the more difficult topics and showed examples from my consulting work.

The last PowerPoint slide winked off the screen at 11:30. I said, "Well if there aren't any questions our class is over." Dead silence filled the room. "Michelle, do you have anything you want to add?" She shook her head no. "Thank you, class, for your attention." The students applauded. That had only happened a few times in my career. I blushed and thanked them again.

Brenda must have heard the clapping. She came in just as I was about to leave. "Thanks again Dan. I am sorry we can't use you anymore."

"No problem, I understand." I looked away, trying to hide my smile. "I'm sure I'll find something. Thanks for the past six months." The last part was sincere.

I almost skipped on my way to the parking garage. When no one could hear me I shouted, "I'm free!" The sunlight glinting off the headlights turned each Ford and Chevy into a smiling co-conspirator.

The worries that plagued me at the start of the week were

distant memories. I was rich and on the way to my airplane, my home, and my family.

I lacked only one thing — someone I could tell about my week. What's the use of doing great things, if you can't talk about them?

"Beth," I rehearsed, "Guess what I accomplished this week. I participated in a drug deal and, in spite of the fact that several people were killed, I have over a half-million dollars in cash. Oh, also, I had great sex with a beautiful woman."

That didn't sound right. I would have to work on what I would and wouldn't tell her.

I loaded the duffle full of cocaine, my computer case (stuffed with over 100, hundred-dollar bills) and my suitcase full of dirty clothes into the back of my plane. I called Beth as I walked up the stairs to the airport's office to pay for my fuel and parking.

"Well, look who's calling. I thought you forgot my number."

"Hi honey, I'm done with class. I'm at the airport in Gaithersburg and should be home in about two hours. What a week, can't wait to tell you about it. How's Amy?"

"Better. She's taking the pain pills. They knock her out. She sleeps a lot. When she's awake, she complains. I'm at the store, what do you want for dinner?"

"Steaks. I'll broil them on the grill."

"Steaks it is. You sound great. You had a good week?"

"I had a great week. Our money problems are over. I'll explain it all when I get home."

"Okay," she responded warily. "Be careful. Call when you land."

"I will. Love ya."

***

The young woman at the fuel counter smiled as I approached. "Did you have a good week, Mr. Goldberg?"

"I did. I had a great week." She handed me my bill. She had an innocent, pretty face, short brown hair, and hazel eyes. She appeared to be in her early twenties. The tag on her shirt let the world know her name — Ashley.

"Will you be coming back next month?"

"Yes, I think so. Will you be here?" *Oh, my God, am I flirting with a girl, just a few years older than my daughter?*

She smiled. "Yep, nine to five, five days a week." Her eyes conveyed a mischievous twinkle. "Do you live far away?"

"Not too far. In Salisbury, Maryland." *Why am I dawdling with her?*

She looked at the computer displaying the aviation weather map. "It looks like you won't have a problem. The wind is from the west at five miles an hour. That's a bit of a tail wind for you. There are reports of a nasty front coming over the mountains, but it won't reach the DC area until midnight. You'll be home by then."

"Great, I'm anxious to get there." Her eyes were captivating. *Was she interested in me or simply bored? I couldn't tell.*

"You must have business here in DC. Are you a lawyer? We get lots of lawyers." Ashley turned away to process my credit card. When she faced me again, the top two buttons of her shirt were undone.

"No, I'm a teacher. I teach statistics courses for government agencies."

"And you're a pilot, lucky you." Scoundrel that I am, I kept my left hand under the counter.

"You know, I've been working here for over a year," she continued, "but I've never been up a small plane. Could you take me for a ride sometime? I mean, if it is not too much trouble."

"Can't do it today. How about next time?"

Her eyes sparkled. Her smile showed all her teeth. "Gee, that'll be great. I'll bring refreshments."

"Ok then, I'll see you in a few weeks — Ashley." She grabbed the receipt from my hand. "Here's my cell number, call me." The back of the receipt now had her name in flowery cursive along with her phone number. She transformed one of the zeros into a smiley face. "Thank you, Dan! I like totally can't wait!"

I walked stiffly down the stairs to my plane. After a while, my heart returned to its normal rhythm.

I did my pre-flight inspection and organized the cockpit just the way I liked it. I needed three charts to transit the controlled airspace and get to my destination. I folded each and fastened them to my clipboard for ready access. It was a routine flight, one that I had done many times. First, I had to get clearance to transit the Washington-Baltimore air space. I knew from experience that the middle part of the day had a lot of commercial traffic. Small, private aircraft are at the bottom of the priority list and often are ordered to delay their departure.

That day was different. Washington control gave me an immediate ten-minute window for takeoff. The controller warned that if I missed the window, I would have to wait at least an hour on the ground. I taxied towards the runway, anxious to get into the air.

Out of the corner of my eye, I saw a car careen into the small parking lot outside the fence. A few seconds later, Ashley's voice came over the radio, "Uh, Mr. Goldberg, there's a woman here for you. She says it's important."

"I'm about to take off. What's her name?" A cold chill went down my spine. In my heart, I knew her answer.

"Maria."

"What does she want?" *I thought we were through with each other.*

"She says she needs to talk to you." There was a pause. "She seems very upset. Should I call the authorities?"

Everyone with an aircraft radio within the surrounding five

miles could hear our conversation. Somewhere, in a windowless FAA facility, the conversation was being recorded for posterity. Most airplane communications are clipped and to the point. Often they have a certain swagger tone that is supposed to convey casual competency. Now my girlfriend's name was broadcast for all to hear.

I had only seconds to make a decision. A twin-engine plane, a Piper Seneca, was heading towards the runway. My plane blocked its path. I had only minutes left before my take-off window would close.

To hell with Maria! She has no claim on me.

But her name brought back memories of our time together. I could hear her laugh, feel her touch, even remember her smell. My hand refused to advance the throttle; my feet refused to release the brakes. Instead, I pressed the microphone button and said: "Ashley, she's my friend. Let her come down to the apron once I park."

I canceled my flight plan with ATC. The Seneca heard this and stopped short on the apron, giving me just enough room to pass, reclaim my parking spot, and shut down the engine.

Maria ran down the stairs carrying a large purse and an overnight bag. She misjudged the last step and fell flat on her face, tearing a hole in the knee of her jeans.

"Dan, Dan, open up!" she shouted when she got to my plane.

"Maria! What the hell are you doing here?" Ashley, all business now, watched us from the top of the stairs, her cell phone in one hand and a portable aircraft radio in the other.

"We have to leave! Now! Don Ricardo and Marcos are dead! They tried to kill me!"

"Don Ricardo and Marcos tried to kill you?"

"No, *estupido!* The men who killed them tried to kill me. We need to go before they get here."

"They know you're here? They followed you?"

"Stop asking stupid questions. We need to leave now!" I looked at her and did nothing. I don't like being told what to do with my airplane. I didn't trust her. She scammed me once. I didn't want to be her patsy again.

"How did you know I would be here?"

"I didn't, I just had to guess. You told me you had an airplane, remember? Besides, I had to warn you!"

I shook my head. "I don't know — "

"Dan, I think they know I'm here. If we don't leave, they'll kill you too!"

Maria's face had changed completely. Long streaks of mascara ran down her cheeks, her hair was a mess; her silk blouse sported a large sweat stain. Crazily, she was never more beautiful to me.

"Stop looking at me. I know I'm a mess. I got a call from Marco's security man an hour ago. He found Don Ricardo's and Marcos' bodies. He was sure that were coming to get me. I packed and got away just in time. Let's go!"

Somehow, the terror in her voice and demeanor overwhelmed my remaining hesitation and hurt pride. "Get in," I said.

We threw my carefully arranged maps, her purse, and overnight bag into the back seat. She was shaking so hard, she couldn't connect her seatbelt. I did it for her and put a set of headphones on her head. I started the engine and announced my plans. "Gaithersburg traffic N-two-three-five tango taxing to the runway for immediate takeoff."

Ashley was still on the balcony. She responded, "Tango, do you want me to contact the authorities?"

"Negative Gaithersburg, I got it. Sorry about the confusion. Tango is rolling toward the runway." I wasn't sure that I believed all of what Maria was saying, but it was clear that we were in this together, at least for now.

I knew that I couldn't request my original flight plan. Besides bringing Maria back to my home airport would be awkward, to say the least. Heading west was our only option.

"Washington Center, N-two-three-five-tango departing Gaithersburg, heading West, VFR."

"Roger, Tango, climb and maintain 2,000 feet. Avoid controlled airspace."

But we couldn't take off. The twin-engine plane that had passed me earlier now had command of the single runway.

"Dan, let's go. What are you waiting for?" Maria asked. She squirmed in the seat, looking towards the parking lot.

"I'm waiting for the plane ahead of us to take off."

"Can't you just pass him?"

"That's an airplane, not a car. It's a runway, not a street. No, I can't pass him."

Not impressed by my lecture, she asked, "Why doesn't he just go?"

"I don't know. He might be waiting for clearance, or he might be checking his engines. For all I know, he might be sitting there talking to — "

Maria screamed. "*Dios Mio,* they're here! Let's go!" She grabbed my shoulder and pointed. A large black SUV braked into the parking lot. "You need to leave. It's them!" Three men got out. One tried to open the gate leading to the apron. When he realized it was locked, he started unpacking a rifle. Two others ran up the stairs to the office. All my considerations about the veracity of Maria's story vanished.

Ashley's voice came over the radio: "Hey, what the hell? You can't bring guns here. No, you can't go out there! Help! …"

The glass door leading from the office to the outside stairs exploded. Ashley stumbled out, blood spurting from a neck wound. She collapsed on the banister rail. The two men followed.

I pressed the microphone button praying that the pilot in the twin was listening. "Piper Seneca at Gaithersburg, this is the Cessna right behind you. Shots have been fired at the office. Departing immediately, using the taxiway to your right."

I didn't wait for a response. I gunned the engine and released the brakes. The Seneca started its roll at the same time. With its two powerful engines, it quickly got ahead of us.

We heard more shots coming from the office. Four black holes appeared on the side of the Seneca's cabin. Over the radio, we heard, "Gaithersburg traffic, Seneca rolling. What? We've been hit! What?"

The big plane slowed. I gained on him. For a moment it looked like my left wing would touch his right wing — a disaster for both of us. I edged to the right as far as I could, my right wheel off the asphalt and on the grass.

"Dan, he's going to shoot," my co-pilot shouted. I turned to see where she was pointing. One of the men had what looked like a high-powered rifle aimed directly at us. I held my breath, expecting an impact.

There was none. "He missed," she shouted. I looked to my left. The bullet hit the Seneca's wing. Aviation gas flowed onto the runway. Another shot. His right main tire exploded, then his landing gear collapsed. The wing burst into flames. The engine transformed the four-bladed propeller into shrapnel.

Deadly pieces flew a dozen feet in front of us. Instinctively, I pulled back the throttle and stepped on the brakes, but not soon enough. A chunk of something hit the left tail section. More shots. More holes in the twin.

"They're trying to kill me," Maria screamed. She unhooked her seatbelt and crouched on the floor. *What about me? God damn it!*

The flaming wreckage swerved to the right, coming towards us. I couldn't stop in time. I didn't want to. Two men with pistols came running our way.

I released the brakes and pushed the throttle all the way in. I had to get airborne.

Slowly, slowly the airspeed needle crept towards the green. The Seneca was still moving towards my path. My engine's RPMs approached red line. Still not fast enough. Maria screamed something in Spanish holding her crucifix to her lips.

The tip of the Seneca's broken wing caught a runway sign in the shallow drainage ditch between the runway and the taxiway. That arrested just enough of its sideway momentum. We were able to pass and get airborne!

The radio exploded with reports of the incident. ATC issued commands, many of them contradictory. I turned off the radio and continued in silence.

I had no idea where we were going. I had no idea where I could land. Looking down, I saw the Potomac River pointing west. Like a trout, I followed it upstream.

"Where are we going," Maria asked. She had climbed out of her hole and re-fastened her seatbelt.

"Where do you want to go?"

"New York. Take me to New York. I have family there. I'll be safe."

"No way. I'm not going there. I need to get home. But first I need to land somewhere and talk to the authorities. I need to explain to the FAA that I had no part of what happened there."

"Dan, you can't go home right now. You can't talk to the authorities. I certainly can't. If you can't take me to New York, let's land somewhere where I can take a shower."

I grabbed my maps from the back seat and searched for a destination. I had enough gas to fly for four hours. That would take me as far west as Columbus, Ohio. But, I wasn't interested in distance. I wanted a nice, quiet location where I could figure out what happened and get rid of my troublesome passenger.

The small town of Cumberland, Maryland seemed like the

perfect choice. "We're going to Cumberland."

Maria said something in Spanish. It contained the name of a barnyard animal, but I wasn't able to understand the verb. She turned away from me, staring blankly into the middle distance. She held a tissue to her scraped knee.

The welcome silence let me resume my connection to the plane. All in all, we (the plane and I) had not done badly. *I'll have to repaint the part that was hit by the debris.*

My plans for the future were as wrecked as the twin engine plane burning on the runway in Gaithersburg. For the first time in my adult life, I had no plans. I had run out of future and was doing my best to hold onto the now.

Chapter 14

On the Lam

I set my GPS and other instruments. My mind shut out the world as I focused on my heading and altitude. Then Maria asked, "Why is that light blinking?"

"That's my transponder. It lets air traffic control know where I'm at. It sends a signal that shows up on their radar." I was in no mood to give her a lesson in navigation.

"Turn it off. Turn it off now!" I ignored her. *Where does she get off telling me how to fly my airplane?*

I didn't respond, and she reached for the control panel. I slapped her hand away. "God damn it, woman, keep your hands off my controls!" I pushed the button to turn the transponder off.

But she wasn't done. "Give me your cell phone."

"Why?"

"They can track us using your cell phone. Give it to me, I'll turn it off."

That seemed reasonable, and I complied. She turned it off and put it into her purse. Her hand came out holding cigarettes and her lighter.

"What the hell are you doing?" I demanded.

"I'm trying to light a cigarette. Can you shut the vent or whatever is making the breeze?"

I slapped her hand a second time. Her lighter flew into the

back seat. "Don't you realize they're 60 gallons of high octane aviation fuel in a 30-year-old tank about a foot above your head? You'll burn us alive." She grunted and reluctantly returned the pack back to her purse. "That was my favorite lighter."

I pressed my advantage. "One more time, how do you know that Marcos and Don Ricardo are dead?"

"Marcos gave each employee a special cell phone to use only in emergencies. We knew that if the phone rang, we had to run. I got the call at nine this morning. Miguel, Don Ricardo's driver, told me that he found their bodies. He said the killers were coming for me."

"Why did you come to me? Why didn't you go to New York or Puerto Rico or somewhere? How am I going to explain this to my wife, to the FAA?"

"I came to you because I didn't know where else to go. The Cartel has contacts at the major airports. They knew my car. Also, Miguel heard the men from the Cartel talking about e*l piloto.* I had to warn you."

"Okay, so you got the call, what did you do?"

"I packed my bag and ran. I knew that you worked at the Parklawn building. I didn't know where in the building and I couldn't get through security, so I waited for you in the parking structure. I waited and waited. I had to pee, but I didn't want to miss you, so I squatted between two cars."

The image of Maria with her pants around her ankles crept into my brain. My face must have betrayed my thoughts.

Maria smiled.

"Go on, what happened," I pressed.

"I went to the top floor and kept an eye on the building entrance. When I finally heard you shout 'I'm free,' I ran downstairs, but by the time I got to your floor, you were gone. I knew you were going to a small airport, but I didn't know which one. Finally, I found someone who told me about Gaithersburg and how to get there." She took a breath. "When are you going to land this thing?"

"In about an hour." I still wasn't satisfied. Maria's story was like a Russian doll. Every time she explained one thing, other questions emerged. Of course, I was hiding things as well. We were a strange partnership.

The Maryland countryside rolled below us. The Potomac, a half-mile wide when we started, had diminished to a lazy stream. We passed over Antietam and Sharpsburg, Maryland the sites of the greatest loss of life during the Civil War. The thought of all that bloodshed did little to put my worries about the blood I had witnessed. *What about Ashley? Did she survive?*

I landed without incident and taxied to a vacant spot at the end of a row of little-used single- engine planes. Before she could unbuckle her seatbelt, I grabbed her arm and said, "What the hell is really going on? There's something you're not telling me."

"They tried to kill me. I got away. Let me go."

"Not good enough. You know something."

An older gentleman came out of the administration building to look at us. I waved acknowledgment. He disappeared back into the building.

"Fuck you, Dan." She reached for the door handle again. I tightened my grip on her arm."

"Ow, that hurts."

"Tell me what you know."

Maria sighed. "Okay, let go of my arm … " I did. She leaned back against the seat.

"Years ago, long before I joined the firm, Marcos imported cocaine, from Columbia and sold it wholesale to dealers in New York. Don Ricardo made him stop when the DEA intercepted one of his shipments. That's when they transformed their real estate business into a money laundering operation. Don Ricardo helped the Cartel buy houses, apartment buildings, and shopping centers earning a healthy commission. It was a good arrangement all around."

"Go on."

"This past Tuesday night a cocaine shipment disappeared. The Cartel thought Marcos stole the drugs and took their revenge. That's all I know."

"Has this ever happened before?"

"That's the crazy part. Mistakes and misunderstandings happen in this business. Deliveries sometimes go bad. In the past, the bosses always worked it out. They never resorted to killing."

"You're sure the gunmen worked for the Cartel?"

"No. Maybe a new group is trying to take over. But Marcos and Don Ricardo are dead, that I know. I would be too if you hadn't saved me." She leaned over in the crowded cockpit and kissed my cheek.

I said nothing. The deaths were piling up: The two men in New Jersey, Henry, Richard, Marcos, Don Ricardo. Maybe Ashley and the pilot of the twin engine plane that burned. Six dead for sure, maybe more. Did my safe deposit box hold enough to justify those lives? Was my soul strong enough?

We got out, and I inspected the plane for damage. The bang we heard taking off was caused by a projectile hitting the tail section. Part of my registration number was missing.

I borrowed the airport loaner car, an old Datsun four-door with a stick shift, and drove into town. On the way, we stopped at a Walmart. Maria bought new jeans and some personal items.

"Give me my phone. I need to call my wife," I said as we got back into the car.

"No, you can't use your phone. The police can trace the call."

"I really need to call my wife."

"Relax, I have another way." I wasn't relaxed. I was pissed-off, and my mood only worsened when she lit a cigarette.

The old man at the airport had recommended the Hilltop Motel. It was the closest accommodation to the airport. I was about to turn in when Maria noticed a Seven-Eleven across the street. "Stop there. They have a pay phone. You can call your wife from there."

"Can't the police can trace a call from a pay phone."

"Not the way I use it." She was quiet as I parked. She bit her bottom lip. She wanted to tell me something. "When you talk to your wife, be sure to tell her to move out of the house."

"What are you talking about? Why?"

"Because she can be a target. If the Cartel finds your name, they can get to you through your wife. They can get to me through you. You're in this. I'm in this. Your wife's involved as well. Is there anywhere safe she can go and take your daughters?"

"I guess they can go to her parents' house. They live in upstate New York. Her father's a big deal lawyer."

"Good. They can afford security."

The pay phone was bolted to the outside wall in full view of the parking lot. A steady stream of Friday night traffic went into and out of the store.

"Write down your wife's cell phone number," Maria demanded. She called a toll-free number then punched in a sixteen-digit code, then Beth's number. "The phone's ringing," she said handing me the receiver. "By the way, you're calling her from Serbia." My accomplice left me on the florissant-lit sidewalk and entered the store.

"Hello, who's this?" Beth said.

"Hi honey, it's me."

"Dan, where are you? Why aren't you home? I called the local airport. They said you haven't landed. I almost didn't answer your call. There's no caller ID."

"I'm calling from a pay phone. I couldn't come home. Something's happened."

"What do you mean something's happened? You okay? Did the plane break down? Don't tell me that we have to spend more money fixing that damn thing."

In the background, through Beth's phone, I could hear our house phone ringing. We still had a land line, although only the girls used it. While Beth continued her harangue, I heard my daughter, Sara, say, "No, he's not here. He's working in Washington. Yes, my mom's here hold on." Then in a voice loud enough to over-shout her mother, "Mom, there's a man on the phone from the FHA or the FFA or something, and he says it's important."

Beth didn't bother to put her hand over the microphone. "Sara, I'm on the phone with you father, tell him I'll call back."

"Dan, why is the FHA calling?" Beth said.

"Sara means the FAA, the Federal Aviation Administration. That's what I was trying to tell you — "

"Mom, did you hear me?" Sara yelled. "Please take this call. I'm expecting a call from Jason! Ask Dad when I'm getting my cell phone."

"Christ, Dan I better take that call. I'll call you back. You better have some answers."

"You can't call me. I'll call you in ten minutes."

I leaned against the wall, breathing hard. I could feel my shirt sticking to my back. Maria stood with a cigarette in one hand and a half-finished beer in the other, oblivious to the "no open containers" sign just over her head. She handed me a cold one from the six-pack at her feet. I joined her truancy with a long, satisfying swallow. "You were listening to my call." *She's taking over my life!*

"Part of it. I'm glad you don't mention my name or where we're at."

"I'm not that stupid. I need to call her back in a few minutes. Will you connect me again?"

"Sure, but first come with me."

She led me to the back of the store, stepping carefully around discarded bottles and other debris. *Am I safe?* I picked up a chunk of broken concrete in case I needed a weapon.

She noticed and said, "Good I'm glad you found something." She laid my cell phone on a set of concrete steps. "Smash it."

"No way, that's my cell phone. It's turned off. No one can find me."

"You're a dumb person with a smart phone. It has a GPS. It can be tracked. Smash it or I will. I'm tired of explaining things to you."

I didn't believe her and tried to get around her to retrieve my phone. She blocked me with her body, grabbed my wrist with both hands, and bit me.

"Ow, damn you!" I dropped the concrete. Maria picked it up and hurled it at the phone. The screen cracked. I pushed her into a pile of trash and turned back to the phone, but she grabbed my ankle. I went down into something brown and slimy. Before I could recover, she crawled back to step and pounded my phone three times. The case broke. The parts flew out. That didn't stop her. She used the concrete rock to pound the broken parts three more times.

Helpless to save my phone I said, "I think you pushed me into dog shit."

"I scraped my knee when you pushed me. It's bleeding again," she countered.

My arm sported a perfect impression of Maria's front teeth, highlighted by a trickle of blood. "Fuck you, you bit me. I'm bleeding."

We lay on the ground, dirty, bloody, and covered with trash. I couldn't help myself. I started laughing. She laughed too. I threw a used condom at her. She threw it back. She crawled over to me and said, "Kiss me, you idiot."

"No, no, go away, you're filthy."

"Kiss me!"

"No," this time with less conviction.

"Kiss me," she purred. We kissed. The world, with all its problems, melted away. We devolved into two mindless organisms, dirty, hurting, bleeding, exchanging saliva as if it was the staff of life itself.

***

"What the fuck? Get out of here!"

We broke apart. A man stood in the open back door. He held a black, bulging plastic bag. Sheepishly, we got up, brushing the dirt off our clothes.

"Sorry," I said. "We're leaving."

He laughed and handed me the bag. "It's okay. You surprised me. Roll around back here as much as you want. Throw this in the dumpster when you're done."

"Let's make your call so we can get back to the motel and clean up. You stink!" Maria said.

"You stink worse!"

"You stink more!" We laughed and hugged each other as we rounded the corner.

Maria held me back before we could get to the pay phone. "When you talk to your wife, let her know she could be in danger."

"What — "

"It will probably take the Cartel a day or so to figure out that I wasn't on the burning plane. Can they trace your plane to where you live?"

"It's possible."

"Tell your wife to leave tomorrow." She used her card to make the telephone connection a second time.

"Guess who called before," Beth said before the second ring.

She didn't pause for a response. "Mr. Oliver from the FAA. He said that you were a witness to a shooting at the Gaithersburg airport. Is that true?"

"Yes, eh, honey, that's what I was trying to tell you before. Three men broke into the airport. They shot the young woman who worked there. They shot up a twin-engine plane. The plane crashed and burned. Do you know if the pilot survived?"

"The pilot and his passenger both died. The clerk died as well. The girls are watching it on TV right now. They're freaking out. Are you OK? How did you get out? Where are you?"

"Oh, my God, I knew the clerk. She was so young." Somehow hearing Beth relay the news made the whole thing worse.

She continued, "Mr. Oliver said you had a passenger in your plane — a woman. Who is she? Where did you take her? Why did you take her? Where, the hell, are you?"

Up to this point, I hadn't really lied to my wife. There were many things I should have told her and didn't, but up to that point, I hadn't really lied.

"I met her at the hotel." *The truth.* "I gave her a ride." *Not the whole truth.* "I had to take off right away and broke some aviation rules." *The truth.* "I'm too exhausted to fly anymore tonight." *More truth.*

"So the FAA is calling to talk to you about some broken rules?" Beth summarized with a hopeful tone in her voice.

"Yes, and they probably want to know what happened from my point of view."

She sighed, "Good. Please call them. Hopefully, they'll revoke your pilot's license, and you'll get rid of that goddamn plane." I could hear the TV news playing in the background. "Dan, where are you? Is that woman still with you?"

"I can't tell you where I am. It's possible that the men who shot up the other plane are recording this call. I'm in danger. It's possible that you and the girls are also."

"Also what?

"Also in danger. Beth, you need to leave. The first thing the morning, go to the place where we had Thanksgiving dinner last year."

"You mean to — "

"Yes, there. Don't say it."

"This doesn't make sense. Why — "

"Beth, the truth is I'm in trouble. I'm in trouble with some very dangerous people. The woman I'm with is trying to help me. I won't be home for several days." I paused and took a breath. *Would I ever come home?* "I no longer have a cell phone. I'll try to call you every other day or so."

"What the hell? What kind of trouble? Did you call the police? Do you want me to call the police? Where are you?"

"I can't give you details. Don't call the police. We don't know who we can trust."

"We?"

"The person I'm with. I need a few days to sort this out. The men who shot up the airport might still be looking for me. It's all a big misunderstanding — "

"Misunderstanding my ass! People don't shoot each other because of a misunderstanding. They — "

"Beth, please listen to me. You need to leave. You and the girls might be in danger."

"You're out of your mind."

"I might be. Right now I need to get off the phone. I'm tired and filthy. You need to pack."

Brief silence then, "She's there with you now isn't she?"

"Yes, but it's not what you think."

"What should I think?"

"Beth, trust me. I need to get off the phone. I'll call you tomorrow."

She was about to say something, but Sara called for her

again.

"Okay, call this Mr. Oliver." She gave me the number and hung up. The were no last words of affection.

Maria was there, a few feet away, lighting a fresh cigarette with the stub of one she had finished. "Very good, you told her nothing."

"Maria, enough! Enough already with the smoking."

She took a final puff and crushed the new cigarette on the sidewalk. "Okay, let's go, we're filthy."

***

A heavy middle-aged woman managed the office at the Hilltop Motel. She might have been pretty once, but too many cigarettes and too much junk food had taken their toll.

"You wanna room for you and your sweetie? Twenty bucks for the afternoon, fifty for overnight."

I could imagine what Maria would say if she knew she was my "sweetie."

"Actually, my *colleague* and I need two rooms for one night," I corrected.

The clerk shook her head. Her double chins wobbled back and forth. "Sure, no problem, two rooms for the night. I'll give you rooms 9 and 10. They're at the end of the row. There's a door between them if you and your eh, *colleague,* want to have a, eh *conference.*"

She chuckled as if she just invented sarcasm. She looked past me, and I followed her gaze. Maria paced back and forth, besides of the car, smoking her third cigarette since landing. Her torn jeans, blood-stained shirt, and messy hair conveyed the image of something other than my "sweetie."

The clerk returned to the task at hand. "That's a hundred bucks cash money. We don't take credit cards. Fill out the registration cards."

The calendar behind her desk provided the inspiration. It displayed a self-satisfied Persian cat sitting on a satin pillow. Black X's showed June more than half gone.

I entered John Katz on one card, June Satin on the other. The two cards and five twenties completed the transaction.

Almost six o'clock. On a normal Friday night, Beth would be preparing dinner. The girls would be playing quietly or reading books. All three would be alert for daddy's footsteps on the porch, triumphant from his successful week in Washington. I wanted that feeling. Instead, I sat in a cheap motel room joined by circumstance to an annoying woman decidedly not my wife.

Maria knocked on the door connecting our rooms. "Why do we have two rooms?"

"Not now. And by the way, you name is June Satin for the evening. I'll explain later."

We showered separately, each in our own bathroom. I knew there was something I had to do but couldn't remember what it was. Exhausted, I dried off and stumbled to the nearest bed and fell asleep.

***

Maria woke me. Dressed in her new jeans and a white t-shirt, she looked like one of my college students.

"What time is it?" I asked.

"Eight o'clock."

"I'm hungry."

"Me too," she said. "We'll eat soon. But right now, come into my room."

"Give me a minute, I'll get dressed."

"No, come now," she insisted.

Did she want to have sex? That was always a possibility with Maria, but her manner was severe, business-like. I wrapped a towel around my waist and obediently followed her. She pointed at the queen-size bed where my cocaine-filled duffle bag occupied pride of place. All its flaps were un-zipped immodestly revealing the illegal contents.

I turned to her, forgetting to hold the towel around my waist. Before I could say anything, she casually brought her right hand from around her back. It held the gun that Richard used to kill the two men.

Our roles changed. She became the prosecutor, I the defendant. The drugs were the evidence. The crime — betrayal. Using the gun as a pointer, she moved it back and forth from the evidence to the naked defendant as she said in a calm but menacing voice, "*Chico*, we need to talk."

Chapter 15

Dan's Confession

Instinctively my hands came down to cover my crotch. I reached for the towel, but she pulled it away.

"The towel won't save you. Go sit in the chair." Once again she used the gun to make her point. Her finger wasn't on the trigger, but I knew that could change.

Where did you get this?" Maria demanded. "Who gave it to you?"

"Let me get dressed, I'll explain." *What should I tell her? What can I withhold?*

"No, explain naked." She came behind me. Put your arms behind your back."

"Don't be ridiculous — Ow." I felt a sharp pain as she tapped my skull with the gun.

"Don't make me hurt you. Put your hands behind your back."

I complied and noticed that the cords that once raised and lowered the blinds were no longer part of the room's inventory. The woman was definitely resourceful. This was the second time she tied my wrists, but unlike the previous night, this time she wasn't playing.

She stood over me. "Does it hurt?"

"Yes, it hurts. You didn't have to hit me."

"Good, I'm glad it hurts." Then in a louder voice, "Where did you get the cocaine?" She pointed the gun at my head, then changed her mind and pointed it at my crotch, then settled on my chest as the best target.

"It's not mine!" *Maybe someone will hear me and come to my rescue.*

"Bullshit. If it's not yours, whose is it?"

"Richard's."

"The taxi driver?"

"Yes."

"Richard's dead. Don't lie to me. Where did you get it?" She slapped my face. I saw the slap coming and turned my head in time to avert most of the blow. Still, it hurt.

Sweat oozed out of every pore of my body. My voice quivered. "He gave it to me for safekeeping before he died. Please untie me. I'll explain."

She ignored my plea. "Explain where you are, naked, tied to a chair in a cheap motel. What would your precious Beth say if she could see you now?"

"Richard hired me to fly him to New Jersey Tuesday night. He told me he had to collect some money from his friend Henry. But he lied to me. It was a drug deal. Two guys ambushed them, killed Henry and wounded Richard. When we flew back, Richard gave me the drugs to hold until he got better. He didn't get better. He died. That's the truth."

"What about the money? If there were drugs, there had to be money."

"Richard gave me ten thousand dollars. He kept the rest." I turned my head away, hoping she wouldn't detect the lie.

"Where is it?"

"Where is what?"

"The money God damn it!"

"In my computer case."

She left the room and returned with my computer case. She

took out the money and stacked the bills on the desk. "There's only ten thousand here. Where's the rest?"

Naked and tied up, I still couldn't tell her the truth. "Richard kept it. I guess he had it in his car when he died."

She spat in my face, walked away, then returned with one of the cocaine packets. "Do you know what this is worth?"

I had an idea but said "No."

"Over ten thousand on the street, half of that wholesale. How much do you think your bag weighs?"

"About 30 pounds."

"That's over six million dollars. You want me to believe that you risked your worthless life for only ten thousand dollars?"

"I didn't know I was getting into a drug deal," I whined. "Otherwise, I wouldn't have done it." I didn't dare tell her that I flew Richard in exchange for a hit of cocaine and one-twentieth that amount.

Her mood softened. "What were you going to do with the drugs? Were you going to sell them?" She laughed at the prospect. She sat on the bed. "Dan, listen to me very carefully. I'm going to ask you some questions. If you don't answer, or if I think you're lying, I'll shoot you in the kneecap. It'll hurt like hell. You'll never walk normally again. Do you understand?"

Her eyes, two dark marbles, penetrated my soul. My entire body quivered with fright. "Yes."

"Now answer my questions truthfully. Do you work for the Cartel?

"No."

"Do you work for the DEA, the FBI, or any other government agency?"

"No!"

"Do you work for a police department?"

"Do I look like I'm a policeman?"

"Answer the question!" She slapped me again.

"No!"

"Did you kill Richard?"

"No!"

"Did you, or your people you work with, kill Don Ricardo and Marco?"

"No! And I don't have people!"

"Did you bring me to this shit-ass motel to kill me?"

"No. You came running to me, remember? I don't work for the Cartel. I don't work for the DEA or the police. Until last Tuesday, I never saw cocaine in my life. I got caught up in this mess because of Richard!"

She pressed the gun barrel into the soft part of my knee until it hurt. "The drugs were in your airplane. Where were you taking the drugs?"

"I was going to dump the bag in the Chesapeake Bay on my way home. I wanted no part of the filthy things."

"Stay there! Shut up! I need to think." She turned away and paced the room. Thankfully, she put the gun on the desk.

"Untie me," I pleaded.

She resumed her seat on the bed. "Let me get this straight. You, Richard and the other asshole decide to take down a Cartel drug delivery. In the process, you killed two of their men. Did you think you would get away with it? How long did it take the two of you to come up with this half-assed plan?"

"It was Richard's plan. I was just supposed to fly him to an airport so he could have his meeting then fly him back. He lied to me, changed airports twice. It rained. I hit one man in the head with my hammer. I shot a gun for the first time in my life. Richard killed both men. We burned their bodies. Please untie me."

"Fuck you, Dan. My friends are dead because of you."

"Fuck you too. You worked for drug dealers."

"Shut the fuck up."

I kept quiet. My inquisitor paced back and forth.

"The Cartel is looking for us," she said more to herself, than, to me. "You really don't know anything, do you?"

"Just what I told you."

"And the rest of the money?"

"Richard kept it."

"You're an idiot."

"Yes." Humility seemed to be the better part of valor.

She sighed and cut my ropes using a knife with the slim blade. I noticed that it was the twin of the one Richard used to arrange his cocaine.

"Relax. I'm not going to kill you. Not today. Get dressed. We really need to talk." She tossed me the towel signaling the end of my inquisition.

I tried to get up, but my knees wouldn't cooperate. "Let me help you," she said transforming from inquisitor to girlfriend.

We stumbled into the bathroom where I sat on the toilet while she tended to my head wound. Every time she touched me I could feel lust replacing anger, pain, and humiliation.

She noticed the growing bulge under the towel and smirked. "Not now *Chico*, I'm not in the mood. Get dressed, I'm hungry. We need cigarettes, beer, rum, and food." I almost said "we" don't need cigarettes, but had the presence of mind to keep quiet.

Once dressed, I walked into the other room. Maria sat at the desk writing on a legal pad she liberated from my computer case. "If the Cartel finds us, we're dead," She said as she handed me the car keys and my wallet. "If we don't either eliminate them or get them off our trail, your family will die."

A cold chill ran down my back. "Look, why don't we go to the police? They'll protect us. We'll give them the drugs and tell them what we know. I'll split the ten thousand with you."

"And then what? Do you really think the police will protect you? Do you think they'll believe your unbelievable story? You were a witness to two murders. Why didn't you go to the police then?"

I had no answer.

"I can't talk to the police," she continued. "Are you that dumb? How do you think I've made my living during these past five years?" She opened the last can of beer and drank. "Get out of here, buy the stuff, come right back."

"Maria, I'm sorry about your friends."

In a calm, sorrowful tone she replied, "Yeah, me too. I need to think about this and what we need to do next. One thing's for certain — you're not dumping the cocaine in the ocean. It's the only thing that'll keep us alive. If we can get to New York, we can sell it wholesale. I have contacts." She took a breath. "With six million dollars, we might get lucky."

She looked at me and said nothing for a few seconds. "Do you know what *cojones* means?"

"Balls?"

"Yes, balls. But it also means courage. Do you have the *cojones* to fly me to New York and help me sell these drugs?"

"Yes, I do." At last a plan! I could feel a whole new life opening up for me. We could sell the drugs, and I'll find a way to get back to Beth and my daughters.

"I need to think. Go buy the stuff. Don't forget the cigarettes. Get a carton." She paused, "I'm sorry I hurt you."

"That's okay. Thanks for the apology."

***

On my way into town, I realized that I left Maria with ten thousand in cash, a gun, and thirty pounds of cocaine. Would she still be there when I returned?

As luck would have it, the liquor store was next to a sub shop. I placed my food order and went next door for the other items.

An older black man and I were the only customers. I bought

a fifth of rum and a six-pack of Corona to the counter where I asked for a carton of Marlboros to complete the purchase. On a whim, I added ten two-dollar "instant" scratch-off lottery tickets. I turned to leave when the other customer advised, "Ain't you gonna check your tickets?"

It was a good idea. *If I win, God's telling me that I'm doing the right thing.*

Three tickets had matching numbers. I handed the winners to the clerk. He ran it through the computer, and said, "You're a winner!" and handed me a hundred-dollar bill. I smiled, looked at the ceiling and whispered "Thanks." No one noticed.

Smiling from ear to ear, I drove back towards the motel with my purchases. Surely it was a sign, but I couldn't discern for what. Despite what I said to Maria, part of me longed for my old life. Her New York drug dealing plan scared me to death.

Part of me wanted Beth. Not the angry, sarcastic woman she had become but the way she was during our honeymoon — a woman who would smoke dope and fuck until she could fuck no more. But she wasn't that woman anymore.

Did I want Maria? The woman, who hit me on the head, tied me up and held me at gunpoint? The woman who rolled in the trash with me, who broke all the rules, who wanted me in the most elemental way? Could we be partners?

I stopped at a red light on the way back to the motel. The road to the right would take me to the airport and my plane. If I took off right away, I could be home before dawn. There would be a lot of explaining, both to the authorities and to my wife, but if I left right away, I could probably save my marriage.

If I turned left, I would return to the motel and Maria. Maybe, the test wasn't from God but from Maria. Maybe, she wanted me to fly home. She'd be rid of me and be able to keep the drugs and money for herself.

Or, maybe she did trust me. I would return, we would talk

and eat and drink and fuck. She would wrap her legs around me, call me filthy names in Spanish and scratch my back while she screamed.

Or maybe she didn't want me anymore. I would return and find Maria, the drugs, and my money all gone.

My left hand held the turn signal lever. If I pressed down, I would turn left to Maria. If I pushed it up, I would turn right to the airport and Beth.

I looked for a sign. *God tell me what to do!* The light turned green. I stayed motionless. Up or down — Beth or Maria. Down or up — Maria or Beth. The light turned red. I had another ninety seconds to make a decision.

I felt the stubs from the winning lottery tickets in my shirt pocket. If God wanted me to go back to my wife, would He let me win a hundred bucks? Was that a sign?

A pickup truck stopped behind me. The light turned green, I didn't move. The driver honked a short, polite honk urging me to make a decision. Turn left or turn right, Maria or Beth. The driver honked again. This time, longer and more urgently. He had places to go, things to do. Maybe he had a woman waiting for him? Didn't the driver know I had to make a monumental decision? Was the pickup truck behind me the sign?

Maybe it was the smell of the subs that tipped the balance. Maybe it was a third honk from the vehicle behind me. Maybe God pressed down on my hand.

I turned left and drove the quarter mile back to the motel.

Chapter 16

Te Amo Tambien

I didn't know what I would find when I got back to the motel.

Maybe she sent me on the shopping trip just so she could leave — taking the drugs and money with her. Maybe she'll be waiting for me, soft, naked, lying on the bed.

I had to tell her what I'd just went through at the stoplight.

Of course, she was angry. Her friends were murdered, she was pursued. No, she'll be there. We'll talk, eat the food, kiss, drink, make love again. This time she'll be gentle.

I found her at the desk, still writing on a legal pad. All business, she glanced at me as if I was the delivery boy. "Light me a cigarette."

"Light it yourself. When are you going to quit smoking? It'll kill you."

She laughed. "I should live so long. I'll quit when I'm good and ready."

I handed her the carton of cancer sticks and a book of matches. "Would you like to eat here or in the other room?"

"We'll eat here. Hand me the booze?"

"What are you working on?"

"I'm trying to figure out how we'll sell this blow."

She had redecorated the room. The cocaine packets now occupied the top of the bureau — twenty neat rows of addiction stacked six high and three deep.

"Where's the cash?" I asked, trying to hide my rising anger.

"I took half. The other half's back in your briefcase." It was as if I asked where I left my bedroom slippers. The cash, like the legal pad and 30 pounds of narcotics, had become community property. I was $5,000 poorer thanks to my aerial hitchhiker.

She opened the rum and took a swig directly from the bottle. "This is shit. Couldn't you get anything better?" She sneered, "And why did you get Camels? You know I like Lucky Strike."

"I thought you — "

"Forget about it. See if you can do something about the temperature. It's hot as hell in here." She lit up and headed to the bathroom. The door stayed open. A moment later, I heard the unmistakable sound of urine meeting water. *Did she leave the door open on purpose? Was it a sign of our intimacy? Or did she care so little about me that it made no difference?*

The window air conditioner in Maria's room was turned up high, but only hot air came out. *Frozen.* I turned it off. The unit in my room wouldn't even turn on. Its power cord ended in three bare wires.

Maria re-entered the room, zipping her fly. "Drink," she said. "You need to drink, even if the stuff you bought is shit."

"No way. We're flying tomorrow. I can't do anything about the heat. Both air conditioners are on the blink."

I needed to share my feelings. I didn't want to talk about alcohol or cooling equipment. I needed to let her know my thoughts at the intersection. Should she know that I was there because of a lottery ticket? But the time wasn't right.

"Drink, we have a long night ahead of us."

"I don't really like rum."

"I don't really like getting shot at. I don't really like spending the night in a fleabag motel in West Nowheresville. We're here. We're in a world of shit." She filled two plastic cups to the brim, grabbed one, tossed her head back and swallowed. I took a sip and put the cup back down on the coffee table.

"This rum really is shit," she said.

"You said that already. I'm tired of your bitching. I'm tired of being ordered around." I grabbed a sandwich and headed for the other room.

"Come *Chico. Lo siento.* I'm sorry. Sit on the bed. Drink, you'll get used to it. I'll eat with you."

We sat and ate and drank. She was right. The rum tasted better after the third or fourth sip. She refilled her glass twice.

She finished half her sub then said, "I'm hot," and pulled off her t-shirt. She took another swig of rum directly from the bottle while trying to chew her food. Some of the liquid ran down her neck and into the cavity between her breasts. Her bra acted as a miniature dam, creating a tiny alcoholic lake.

"Whoops! *Estoy poco borracha.* I'm a little drunk. Come, *Chico*, take a drink." She added an extra ounce directly from the bottle to make an effort worthwhile and shook her chest back and forth. Unable to resist, I buried my face between her breasts and slurped a wild combination of booze and sweat. I started to unfasten the button securing her jeans, but she pushed me away with a giggle. "Not now, *Chico*, we need to talk."

I found a towel and wiped my face. "Okay, let's talk." I handed her the towel. She wiped her chest.

"So tell me, *Chico*. What were your plans today?"

"I was going to fly home to my family and throw these filthy drugs into the bay. I want no part of them.

"And the money?"

I shrugged. "My daughter needs new braces. We have credit card bills to pay."

"And then what?"

"And then *nada*, nothing. We, you and I, our relationship was over. I was going to live my life, teach my classes. My younger daughter broke her arm this week. My older daughter wants a cell phone. My lawn needs mowing."

She nodded her head like a prosecuting attorney leading a witness into a confession. "So you were going to go home and mow your lawn and forget about me and the drugs that you stole from the Cartel?"

"I didn't steal — "

"Oh, right. You and your friend Richard just found the drugs and the money. Do you really think the Cartel cares about that detail?" Maria finished her shot and poured another. Great, I thought, I'm in an isolated hotel room with a woman guzzling rum. I didn't see the gun but suspected she hid it within easy reach.

She put her glass down and leaned over to me. Holding both my hands, she stared intently into my eyes. "Do you really think the people you stole from will forget about their drugs and their money? Now that they know you and I are together, they will use your family to get to you, they will use you to get to me. Whether you like it or not, you, me, your family, we're all in this together." She paused, sipped more rum.

"They would go after my family?"

"*Por supuesto!* Of course! It will take them some days to figure out the connection and your address, but it will happen. Can you imagine what the Cartel goons would do to your daughters?"

"Oh, my God — "

"You sent them away, right?"

"I told my wife to go to my father-in-law's."

"Good."

We were silent for a few minutes. We saw a flash of lightning and heard thunder. The rainstorm was on its way.

"I didn't steal the drugs. We only took them and the money after two assholes tried to kill us!"

She laughed, and a mouthful of rum sprayed across the bed-covers.

Even as I said the words, I realized it was a ridiculous argument. I imagined coming before Pablo Escobar in a jungle courtroom trying to explain the distinction between stealing drugs and appropriating them after a fight. *Your honor, my co-defendant and I are innocent. We didn't mean to steal the drugs.* I shuddered to think how the jury would react.

Back from the jungle, I said, "Can't we just return the drugs to the Cartel?"

"Dan," she said carefully pronouncing each syllable, "You really are an idiot." She pointed to the cocaine. "Do you think this is like a library book that you can return and pay a fine?"

If I were back in Escobar's courtroom, I would stand and object. "Your honor, the prosecution is using an unfair metaphor." I couldn't resist the weight of her logic and fell silent.

Maybe Richard and Henry were the bad guys? Maybe the two dead men were federal agents? I only had my co-conspirator's explanation, and he had certainly proved to be unreliable. My mind whirled. Maybe the bad guys were the good guys? Maybe I was one of the bad guys?

Something in my mind shifted at that moment. I came to realize that Maria, with all her faults, wasn't a wall keeping me from my former life. She was the bridge into whatever life awaited me. Was *this* the sign I was looking for? I couldn't go home. I would never mow that lawn again. At that moment I surrendered to Maria and our mutual fate.

Maria leaned over to me and held my head gently. "*Chico,* you can't go home. Someone else will have to mow your lawn." It was as if she was reading my mind.

"Are they watching my house?"

"They might be."

Maria got up and looked at herself in the mirror. The suave, well-dressed, confident business woman I met on Monday night was gone. Her hair was a mess. There were dark circles under her eyes. Sighing, she took off her bra. "We can't talk to Cartel or to the police. If we can sell the cocaine, we have a chance. We leave first thing in the morning."

"I'll be a fugitive. I'll lose my pilot's license."

"That's what you're worried about? Do you want to live? Do you want your family to live? Once we sell the cocaine, we'll have power. Now, we have none. Enough! I'm not going to try to explain it to you, *estúpido*. You figure it out. I'm taking a shower."

My confusion, worry, and concern for my family melded into a witches' brew. Sautéed over a fire fueled by lust, exhaustion, and too much rum, the mixture fermented and turned into desperation.

Desperation can do strange things. It can bring people together and can tear them apart. When Sara was one-year-old, she had a life-threatening infection. We rushed her to the hospital for treatment. That night Beth and I lay next to each other trying to sleep, worrying if the new medicine would do the job and if our daughter would recover. Strangely, it was the loneliest night of my life. We lay there one foot apart, each in our own personal hell.

This time, desperation morphed into a kind of love. From the depth of these emotions I said, "Maria, I love you."

She turned just as she stepped out of her jeans and asked, "What did you say?

I couldn't believe it myself. The words lingered in the air like her cigarette smoke. "I said I love you."

She looked directly into my eyes. "Say it again."

"I love you."

"In Spanish, we say, *te amo.* Say it in Spanish."

"*Te amo.*"

She nodded and said, "*Yo te amo también.* I love you too, you crazy, stupid, horny gringo."

We kissed. The rum on her tongue ran down my throat. The sweat from her armpits filled my nostrils and mixed with the smell of my fear and desperation. We were hot, worried, dirty and exhausted. We were a little drunk. In spite of it all — in spite of the gun, the cocaine, my cell phone in the trash, and the horrible names she called me — I wanted her. I wanted her in a more complete way than I ever wanted a woman in my life. I buried my head in her chest and hugged her with all my might.

We fell onto the bed. I cried. She sensed my wordless need and offered her breast. I found the nipple and sucked. She stroked my head while whispering soothing words in Spanish.

I sucked her nipple as if in sucking I could extract her essence. I sucked seeking the affirmation I wasn't a bad man — I wasn't the author of heartbreak and death.

At its start, the embrace wasn't sexual — it was a quest for comfort, for security, for sanity in what had become a rapidly changing world. But, in the end, a breast is a breast, and when her nipple became engorged, Maria broke the hold. She held my head in her hands. "*Chico*, I have no idea how this will end but remember, you are mine."

We kissed deeply, and in a flash, we were making love. Or rather I was making love. Maria lay on her back and drew me in, providing the safe place I needed. As my passion mounted, her hips moved with mine, then she whispered, "Now, *Chico*."

It was quick. I was selfish. I didn't care. I needed her. She was there for me.

Chapter 17

Maria's Story

I fell asleep in Maria's arms and woke to the sound of thunder. The clock displayed 3:00 a.m. She slept next to me, snoring quietly, wearing one of my t-shirts.

I recalled our last conversation as I showered in the adjoining room. We said, "I love you." We said it in two languages. I said it three times. My mind raced.

What did we really mean? What about my wife and daughters? Who was Maria, really? Was she ever married? Did she have children? Maybe, even now, it wasn't too late. Maybe, I could sneak out before she wakes up.

That plan dissolved as soon as I opened the bathroom door. Maria sat against the headboard smoking a cigarette, staring at the rain.

"Good morning."

"Good morning, aren't you tired?" I asked.

"No, if you want to sleep, use the other room."

There was a brusque, officious tone to her voice. Maybe she had her own early morning doubts. I just stood there, ashamed of my mutinous thoughts. She noticed my hesitation. "If you don't want to sleep, we can watch TV."

"No, let's talk."

"Haven't we talked enough?"

Her eyes, free of makeup, drew me in. Any thought of leaving vanished. "I want to know more about you. How did you meet Don Ricardo? Were you ever married?"

She lit a fresh cigarette with the butt of the one in her hand. Her eyes followed the smoke as it drifted toward the partly open window.

"I never married. Besides one teenage crush, you are the only man I ever said *te amo* to." She turned to me, her voice hard and flat. What you really want to know is, 'how did I end up working as a hostess?' I can see it in your eyes."

"Yes, that too." The wind shifted. I closed the window to keep the wet outside and pulled on a pair of briefs.

She looked at me critically. "When we get to New York, I'm gonna upgrade your underwear collection. White isn't your best color."

She poured more rum and took a breath.

"Mama, Roberto, Teresa and I arrived in New York in July. We found a comfortable, three-bedroom apartment in in the Spanish-speaking section of Queens."

"Did your mother ever learn English?"

"Except for some of the numbers and a dozen other words she never did. She died last year. But I'm getting ahead of the story."

"Sorry."

She got out of bed and started pacing. "Soon after we arrived, I fell in love with my cousin, Victor. He was seventeen and very handsome. I was thirteen, awkward, and inexperienced. He volunteered to show me the city. He was my first lover."

"Did he care about you?" I could feel my pulse quicken at the thought of an innocent thirteen-year-old being used for sex. It made me think of my own daughters.

"Not really. I soon found out he had another, prettier, girlfriend."

"The bastard."

She swallowed more rum. "It wasn't such a big deal. High school was. Learning English, having to think about everything I wanted to say, was a pain in the ass. I hung out with other Latinas. We learned English by watching soap operas."

"That worked?"

"It worked great. We taped the episodes then we would each take a role. We acted all the parts — even the male roles. We'd do it over and over until we got it right. Sometimes we would perform for our relatives."

"Very creative," I said.

She blushed.

"So, go on."

"Okay, so I'm in high school and my body's filling out. Boys started to notice me. I had lots of boyfriends. I even dated the football team's quarterback. He took me to the prom my senior year."

"Was he one of your lovers?"

"Two horny teenagers, what do you think? It was sort of the price of admission. Are you jealous? Don't worry, I didn't love him. The last I heard he weighed 300 pounds." Some ash dropped off the end of her cigarette onto the sheet.

"Did your mother work while you were in high school?"

"I feel like I'm being interrogated. No, she didn't work. We had the money from the insurance, and from the house, we sold in Puerto Rico. Uncle Julio managed Mama's finances. They set aside a certain amount for Roberto's college. The rest went into Julio's clothing business. He paid the rent and gave Mama cash every month. My sister went to work as his bookkeeper."

"It sounds like your family adjusted to the tragedy and the move rather well."

Maria shook her head. "The crash came a month after I graduated high school. Julio's real business was importing and distributing heroin. The clothing business was a front. Theresa flew to Panama every month; supposedly check on Julio's factory. Each time she brought back drugs in her body cavities. The DEA busted her at the airport."

"That's horrible! Did they arrest Julio?"

"They never got the chance. Someone shot him in the head the same day." She took a long drag on her cigarette and closed her eyes."

"Who killed him?"

"I don't know. Maybe it was the same people you ripped off, the ones that tried to kill me. Maybe there's a kind of justice." She smiled as she paced back and forth. I caught a glimpse of her white panties every time she took a turn.

"He was a real son-of-a-bitch. My sister went to prison. Roberto dropped out of college. Now he drives a taxi during the day and plays trumpet in a band some evenings. We'll go hear him when we get to New York."

"Is your sister still in jail?"

She shook her head and started to weep.

"Maria ... "

"Not now." She turned around and went to the bathroom. I heard all the usual sounds, only partly drowned out by the storm. I waited patiently until she emerged.

"What happened to your sister?"

"She's dead. She died in prison in less than a year ... Heroin overdose. Maybe Julio got her hooked. Maybe, she got hooked in prison. I'll never know. She changed in prison — became hard, cynical."

I held her. She rested her head on my shoulder. I rubbed her back. She stopped crying.

"Do you want to hear the rest of my story?"

"Do you want to tell it?"

"Yes, I think it helps."

She took another sip of rum and continued.

"After Julio died we had little savings and no money coming in. Mama and I moved into a cheaper, one-bedroom apartment near JFK. I lied about my age and got a job at Macy's. I worked as a waitress at a sleazy diner at night. That's where I started trading sex for money."

She turned away from me and took another sip of rum.

"Roger was my first. He ate his supper at the diner three nights a week. We chatted when business was slow. One night he asked if I would like to meet him in his car after my shift. At first, I refused. But Mama needed new glasses, and the rent was due. The third time he asked, I agreed. He seemed harmless enough.

"When we got to his car, he put a fifty-dollar bill on the dash without saying a word. I stared at the bill. My tips for a six-hour shift were only half of that. He pushed his seat back and opened his pants. I followed his directions and pretended to be excited. It lasted only a few minutes."

"Was it awful?"

Maria shrugged. "The act wasn't half bad and nothing that I hadn't done before with my boyfriends. Cleaning the diner's toilets was much, much worse. Roger thanked me profusely. I never got thanks for cleaning the johns. That month, we were able to pay our rent on time.

"Roger and I repeated the scene about once a week. We became friends. He referred me to some of his co-workers. Soon, I was making several hundred dollars a week."

Maria filled her glass with the last of the rum. "Do you really want to hear this? Do I disgust you?"

"No, I want to understand where you were coming from. Did your mother know what you were doing?"

"No, she just thought I was getting big tips. In a way, I guess I was."

"Bad joke."

Maria shrugged and lit another cigarette. "Are you sure you

want to hear this? This is the first time I've ever told anyone."

I took her in my arms. Her hair smelled of smoke. "I want to hear it all."

She wiped away a tear and continued. "I stopped waitressing but kept my job at Macy's. I upgraded my wardrobe, hair, and makeup.

"I met Don Ricardo about half a year later. We sat at the same table at my cousin Nelda's wedding. He was very well dressed and had rings on almost every finger. He seemed interested in me, and I thought he might become a client. At the end of the evening, he gave me his card and asked me to come to his office.

"When I arrived, I found Don Ricardo, his son, Marcos and his comptroller, Arturo. After introductions, Ricardo had me sit while he read from a file folder. No one spoke for five minutes."

"That must have been scary."

"Yes, it was. Finally, he closed the folder and looked at me with sad eyes. He expressed sympathies to my family regarding the tragedy in Puerto Rico. He asked polite questions about my work at Macy's. Then he said, 'Now to your other business — we understand that you occasionally have sex with men in exchange for money.'"

"Oh, my God. He just blurted that out?" I interrupted her.

"Yes, he did. Then he said, 'The organizations that control the sex industry in New York deal harshly with competitors. You could be in danger. I say this without moral judgment, only as one business person to another.'"

"He had you investigated. Did you think about leaving?"

"I freaked. My face turned bright red. Every pore in my body released sweat. I just about peed in my dress. Ricardo spoke quietly into an intercom, and a receptionist brought me a tall glass of ice water.

"I finally found the courage to ask, 'Am I in danger Don Ricardo?'

"He shrugged, raised the shoulders of his Italian-made suit, and said: 'Prostitution is a dangerous business. You've been lucky thus far, but you must stop at once.'

"I nodded yes. He wasn't done.

"'Yet you must earn a living, and the pay at Macy's can't support you, your mother, and your sister once she's released. The wedding made us relatives. I'm taking your family under my protection. But you must abide by my rules.'

"'Your rules, Don Ricardo?'

"'You must stop your prostitution and work for me.'

"'Work for you, Don Ricardo?' I'm sure I sounded like a demented parrot."

Maria went quiet for a few minutes. I wasn't sure what to say.

"You were under terrible stress," I offered.

"You're not kidding," she said and went on again.

"I quit working at Macy's and went to work at Don Ricardo's firm. I started as a telemarketer getting leads for manufactured homes in Florida and passing them on to the agents. I did well. Once I passed the test and got my Realtor license, I sold real estate in Queens and Brooklyn working mainly with Spanish-speaking clients. Three years ago, I started working with overseas investors. At first, it only involved being a guide and translator. Soon, the macho South and Central American clients wanted other, more intimate services, and Don Ricardo made it clear to me that those services were part of the job."

I snickered. "So prostitution was a dangerous business when you were your own boss, but not when you worked for him… "

Maria smiled a little. "Don't be cynical. I was always allowed to say no. Sometimes I did. More often I didn't. I found that when I said yes, the deals seemed to conclude faster and at a higher price."

She was done. I said nothing for a while. The sky had changed from black to gray. The rain came down in steady sheets.

"Wow, that's quite a story," I said finally. Then, out of nowhere the hurtful part of my mind added, "Do you have children?"

Her face clouded over. She crossed her arms in front of her chest. "Despite all the fucking, I was never pregnant."

That started her talking again. "Some of Don Ricardo's clients had really fascinating personalities. Some of my assignments were exciting. I really enjoyed working with them and only rarely felt that the intimate services were a burden."

She took a breath. "You need to know, I've only been in love with two men — Victor and you."

The word love came back into the room and hung there like her cigarette smoke. She said she loved me.

"There you have it. That's how I became a hostess in a company that no longer exists."

We both said nothing. The rain, pounding on the roof, provided the soundtrack for the end of her story.

"Let's get dressed," I said. "We need to leave."

"In a minute." She pulled a piece of paper from her purse. "I found this in your briefcase … "

"You went through my briefcase?"

"Yes, I went through your briefcase. I'm wearing your t-shirt. Some your sperm are still swimming in my body. We're a couple, Dan. We can't have secrets. It's about time you accepted that."

"Yeah, still … "

"Now back to this receipt. You rented a safe deposit box the day after you flew to New Jersey to get the coke …"

"I didn't fly there to get drugs. Richard tricked me."

"Whatever. Your idiot friend took the money and left you the drugs. That's what you told me. Are you sure Richard had the money in his car when he died?"

She held the waved the receipt in my face. It was time to surrender.

"I lied. Richard gave me the money as well as the drugs. He told me to hold it until he got better. If he didn't, I was to give half to his sister in Jamaica and keep the rest."

"Now we're talking. How much money, Dan?"

"Just over $600,000."

She slapped my face, "Don't lie to me, you son-of-a-bitch. There is no way anyone would sell that much coke for 600 grand."

"We might have left another bag in the car."

"What car?" Maria asked.

"The car we burned with the bodies."

"What bodies?"

"Henry's and the two guys who attacked us."

"You burned more than a half-million dollars in cash?"

"I think so."

She slapped my face again. I was getting used to it.

"Are we in this together or not? Tell me now. No more lies."

"No more lies." I nodded, trying to make her see I was sincere.

"Are you sure?"

"You and me. No more lies."

"What were you going to do with the cash in the bank?"

"I was going to take about ten thousand out each month until I could find a job. It was going to support my family for at least five years. That's before I rescued you at the airport. Now, somehow, I need to get it to my family. If I'm with you, it means I can't be with my family. I owe them something."

Maria nodded, turned her back, and started putting on her clothes. I did the same. By the time we were both dressed, she had a solution.

"Okay, the money should go to your wife. It would be nearly impossible for us to get it anyway. Write your wife a letter. Don't go into a long story about love and all that. Keep it business-like.

The truth is you're toxic. You're too dangerous to be with your family.

"Tell your wife how to get the money and enclose a key and the receipt. Once we sell the drugs, we'll go to Jamaica and give Richard's sister her share."

"What do we do when the money runs out?"

"We'll think of something else. You're smart. It time for you to get creative."

We found a truck stop not far from the airport. While Maria bought food and water, I mailed the envelope to my wife at her parents' address. My hand shook as I dropped the envelope into the mailbox. I tried not to think about Beth's face when she opened the envelope. I could imagine what her father would say. Would I ever see my daughters again? Would they hate me?

"All done?" Maria asked.

"All done."

"Let's fly."

Chapter 18

Flying Blind

We left the motel at six in the morning on the longest day of the year. The rain continued unabated. The car radio offered no encouragement: "The east coast from Savannah, Georgia to Boston is socked in. There's a hundred percent chance of rain — heavy at times. Many flights are canceled or delayed."

Maria looked worried. "Can we still fly?"

"Yes, I'll file an IFR flight plan."

"What's that?"

"I go to the FAA website and fill out a form that tells them where we're going and how we'll get there. We'll be in clouds the whole way. Don't worry. I have an autopilot. It won't be hard. I've done this before. It might be scary at first because you won't be able to see anything out the window. We'll be flying blind."

"You've done this before?"

"Yes. Trust me."

Maria lit another cigarette and made the sign of the cross.

"Does that help?"

"It can't hurt."

We parked in the designated spot at the airport. Before I could get out of the car, Maria said, "I never wanted to break up your marriage. This week has been a royal fuck-up from beginning to end."

"I know."

"Do you regret meeting me?"

"I regret hurting my wife and kids. That will stay with me the rest of my life. I'm not spiritual, but somehow I feel you and me were meant to be together. You get me. Even when we fight, we fight in a more meaningful way. Bottom line, lady — you're stuck with me."

"You didn't mention our sex together."

"That was, … that is amazing. I've been thinking of things I want to do with you when we get to New York."

Maria smiled. "I can think of some things as well. How long will it take to get there?"

"About three hours. A lot depends on the weather."

"And you're sure we'll be safe?"

"Absolutely."

Maria started laughing as we waited at a light.

"What's so funny?"

"It's really funny *Chico, Muy rico.* Do you know about *Narcocorridos*?"

"No."

"*Narcocorridos* are ballads about the Mexican drug gangs. They celebrate the cleverness of the gangs and ridicule the stupidity of the police. They're all the rage in Mexico and in the border states. As soon as your story gets out, someone will write a *narcocorrido* about a clueless college professor and how he took down a drug deal worth millions of dollars. The Cartel won't be amused. Aye, *Chico, estamos en un mundo de mierda* — we're in a world of shit."

I broke the depressing silence. "Let's get out of here."

***

The clouds hung about two-hundred feet over the runway. Maria transferred our luggage into the plane while I went to the office to pay for the fuel. The sole employee was surprised to see me. "You didn't need to bring the car back so soon. I don't expect you'll be flying in this soup."

"Actually, I need to get going. Did you fill both tanks?"

"Yep. Here's the bill. You sure you want to fly? The weather service says there's fog and rain all up and down the east coast. They're predicting the rain will come again real soon."

"We'll be fine. I'll just file an IFR flight plan."

"Suit yourself. The computer's over there."

The flight plan form asks for the pilot's name, the plane's tail number and details regarding the origin, destination, altitude, and route. I thought about entering false information, but there were too many ways to get it wrong. Not all pilots or airplanes are IFR certified. On the other hand, I was worried that the FAA might have published some sort of all-points alert for my plane. Suppressing my anxiety, I entered the truth then pressed the enter key. The approval came back immediately. I had fifteen minutes to get off the ground and into the air.

I ran back to the plane just as the annoying drizzle turned into a downpour. Maria read the checklist.

"Set radio frequencies."

"Check, frequencies set to the common airport frequency and FAA control."

"Set altimeter."

"Check." I turned the knob, so the altimeter matched the airport altitude.

"Set transponder."

"Check." I entered the code from the website.

I pressed the radio button and announced, "N Two Three Five Tango departing runway ten, heading east."

The old man in the office responded. "Read you loud and clear Tango. Have a safe flight."

Even then, I could have changed my mind. Richard-like, I could have turned to Maria and said, "Me plans dey be changed," but I didn't. I was caught like a leaf in a swiftly flowing stream.

I released the brakes. Maria put her hand over mine. Together we advanced the throttle and started to roll.

Seconds later our tires left the pavement. I pressed the microphone button and said, "Morgantown Center, this is Cessna N Two Three Five Tango, airborne out of Cumberland, Maryland, IFR to Caldwell, New Jersey."

The controller replied: "Roger, Tango climb and maintain 7000, proceed en route."

We continued to climb. First, the cars disappeared, the smaller buildings followed then the trees. For a moment only the church tower peeked through the haze — a narrow, wooden island in a white sea of fog. Then it disappeared as well.

Maria held her crucifix and muttered a prayer in Spanish as the clouds closed in.

It's hard to convey the sense of spatial confusion while flying blind. Normally we depend on outside clues to let us know which way is right, left, up, or down. There are no visual cues in the clouds. My instructors taught me not to look for any. Pilots, who look outside their cockpits while flying blind, often end up as morbid statistics.

I had to do four things at the same time. Maintain the proper heading to the next waypoint, stay within one hundred feet of the assigned altitude, calculate the heading to the next waypoint, and communicate with ATC. That's a lot. That's why, over my wife's objections, I used one of our credit cards to purchase a $10,000 autopilot. It manages the first two tasks, leaving me free to handle the rest.

I clicked the button marked "ON." Normally, a green light would blink four times, then the servo motors would take control of the yoke. This time the red "FAULT" light illuminated. I turned the device off, then on again, pressing the button more forcefully. *Come on you expensive hunk of junk. Take over!*

The extra force didn't make a difference. The "FAULT" light stayed on. I would have to fly by hand.

"Shit. The autopilot isn't working. I need you to help."

"I don't know anything about flying an airplane. You said that you knew what you were doing. Let's land and rent a car."

"Calm down. We'll be okay. Take a breath."

"*Dios mio.* What the fuck have I gotten into."

"We'll be fine. Your job is to keep the plane at 7,000 feet. If we lose altitude, pull up on the yoke. If we go up by more than a few feet, push down. Do it gently. I'll be here to help."

"How do I know if we're at 7,000 feet?"

"You have two gauges. This one tells you the altitude. This one tells you your rate of climb or descent. Try to keep it at zero. If you see that we're climbing, push down. If you see that we're going down, pull up. That's all you need to do."

"That's all I need to do. What will you do?"

"Everything else."

"*Madre de Dios.* She put her shaking hands on the controls. "I'll do the best I can."

"Don't worry. I'll help."

I took responsibility for the heading, navigation, and communication. Fortunately, there was almost no wind. We were able to fly almost directly to each waypoint without having to correct for a crosswind.

As I crossed each waypoint, I contacted the appropriate control facility, checked in and let them know my estimated time of arrival at the next waypoint. I tracked our progress on the chart in my lap. We were heading almost directly east toward Smyrna, Delaware where I planned to turn north towards New Jersey.

Other pilots in other airplanes followed the same route. We were an airborne community, each depending on the others to stay alive.

***

Just west of Smyrna and forty-five minutes into our flight, ATC announced: "Cessna N Two Three Five Tango, you are hereby directed to change course immediately and land at Dover Air Force Base. Descend to 2000 feet, now. Turn left and head north. We have you on radar and will direct you to runway ten. Acknowledge."

That type of announcement was reserved only for hijacking and national emergencies. I knew the police would be waiting. I tried not to show my panic.

Before I could respond, Maria asked, "What does that mean? Do we have to land?"

"Yes, they want to talk to us."

"It's the police, right?"

"Yeah, I guess they found us."

"Do something! They'll throw us in jail."

"There's nothing I can do. They have us on radar. We better dump the cocaine."

"No fucking way! Anyway, they'll find traces all over us and in the plane."

ATC broadcast again. This time the speaker had a deeper voice. "Cessna N Two Three Five Tango, you are directed to change course and land immediately. Click your microphone twice if you can't respond."

Maria slapped my hand away from the controls. "Dan, we're not gonna land. I'm not going to prison. My sister died in prison. I'll kill myself first."

My finger hesitated over the transmit button.

The FAA controller repeated the order: "Cessna, did you copy? You are instructed to land now!"

Maria turned off the radio. The woman was a quick learner.

"What are you doing?" I yelled. "We have to land. That was an order."

"Fuck their order. We're not landing. I'm not talking to the cops. I'm not going to prison. Think of something."

I ignored her protests and reduced power. I would use my GPS to find the airport.

"No," Maria shouted. She pushed the yoke all the way forward. The plane pointed toward the Delaware farmland at a sixty-degree angle. *We're gonna die.*

The plane spun clockwise. I felt like throwing up.

"Maria, we're gonna crash!"

She didn't respond.

Our airspeed crept close to the red line. Over the red line, planes can lose their wings.

We passed six-thousand feet in a blink of an eye. Then five-thousand, then four-thousand. Only dumb luck kept us from hitting other aircraft.

"We're not landing at some fucking Air Force base!" she screamed.

I pulled the yoke up with enough force to overpower her. We leveled out. She let go. We started to climb. Tears streamed down her face. She looked like a cat cornered by a pit bull at the end of an alley.

"Maria, it's okay. We'll be okay."

"No, it's not okay. I'm not going to prison!"

She pushed her seat back. *Thank God. She's letting me take over.*

Then she lifted her knees to her chest.

"No, Maria, don't!"

She positioned her sneakers firmly against the yoke. I knew what was coming and pulled up with all my might. She pushed down with her strong leg muscles. Our airspeed dropped. The stall horn sounded.

"Okay, okay, we won't land," I shouted. "Let go. For Christ's sake, please let go!" We were at less than two-thousand feet —

still in the clouds.

Maria looked at me to judge my sincerity. Finally, she returned her feet to the floor.

I added power, leveled out and headed east toward the Atlantic Ocean, staying at 2,000 feet. *Time to be creative.* I turned the transponder dials to 1600.

"What are you doing?" Maria asked.

"Code 1600 is used for airplane hijacking. ATC will think we've been hijacked."

"I don't understand."

"They've been tracking us since we took off from Cumberland. We didn't comply with their orders and turned off the radio."

"Don't forget our aerial tug-of-war."

"Yeah, that too. ATC will think there's a third person in the plane. We struggled, tried to land. He overpowered and made us head east."

"Sexist pig! What can't our hijacker be a woman?

"Okay, she overpowered us."

"That's better. How does the transponder fit in?"

"That's the clever part. Our hijacker doesn't know about airplanes. I was able to enter the code."

"Ok, I follow. Our imaginary bad person is in the back seat with a gun to our heads. What's next?"

"He or she will kill us. We're going to die."

"The imaginary person will shoot us?"

"Not exactly. The person will do something to make us crash into the ocean. It'll be very sad."

"How does that help?"

"Our deaths will get both the Cartel and the federal agencies off our backs."

Maria thought for a moment. "You do have a plan B in mind, right?"

"Yes."

She extended her hand for a high-five. "Bravo! See, I knew you could use that over-educated brain of yours. Let's go die!"

***

I tried to imagine the chaos we created at the air traffic control. Someone would call the Cumberland airport. They would try to call me. They'll probably call my wife. I didn't think they would scramble Air Force jets to shoot us down. At least, not as long as we were over land. Once we were over water, all bets were off.

About fifteen minutes after our aerial tug-of-war, my GPS showed we were now over the ocean. I stayed at 2,000 feet, just low enough to stay off any land-based radar

We said nothing as the miles clicked by. The fuel gauge showed the tanks at just under three-fourths full. We could fly for three more hours.

When we were twelve miles away from land, I reduced power to idle and descended towards the waves. If the clouds continued to the surface, we would drown.

I kept my eyes locked on the altimeter. At five hundred feet, I said, "Please look down, and tell me what you see."

"I see nothing."

Four hundred feet — "What now?"

"I still see nothing. I'm scared."

My concentration shifted. I thought about how my family would feel when some official told them I died. A puddle of sweat formed in the small of my back.

The stall horn sounded. I lost concentration and let my airspeed drop.

I added more power, using more fuel. The horn silenced.

Three hundred feet. "See anything?"

"I see something."

I looked out, and sure enough, I saw the green, cold waves of the Atlantic through a hole in the clouds. Then the clouds closed in. I ventured lower.

We finally broke through at one hundred feet. The clouds formed a ceiling above us as we flew at the height of an eight-story building. There were no landmarks, just endless water below and the endless clouds above.

We still headed east. If I had the fuel, we could reach Europe in about twenty-four hours. Lindbergh did it with a less capable plane.

My flight instructor's voice came back to me — *"Stay in the present. Don't think about what might happen. Don't think about the mistakes you've made, the things you should have done, the things you might have done. Just deal with what is happening at the moment. Use your training and all the resources at your command."*

One hundred and fifty pounds of resources sat in the passenger seat to my right.

"Maria, you need to fly the plane."

"Some other time. Just get us back to land. We need to get to New York."

"This is important. Just put your hands on the controls and keep the plane steady. You can do it. You've done it before."

"Yes, but we were way up in the air. What if we go down?"

"You can do it. Don't worry about the heading. Just keep the plane at this altitude."

"*Dios mio.* Okay, like this?"

"That's perfect. Whatever you do, don't go down."

"I'm not an idiot."

I released my seat belt and retrieved Maria's suitcase. "Hey, what are you doing with my things?" She let go of the yoke. We started to dive.

"Pay attention!" I grabbed the yoke, pulled up, and brought the plane back to level. "Take over! Keep us at 100 feet."

"*Sí, mi Comandante!*"

"What did you say?"

"Never mind. When we get to New York, you'll need to learn Spanish."

I gathered a bundle of her clothing into my lap. The next part was tricky. It's not easy to open an airplane door in flight.

"Maria, turn the plane slightly to the left," I added power. We tracked a tight circle over some desolate spot in the Atlantic. The left turn reduced the air pressure against my door.

I leaned against the door and released the lock. Chaos erupted. The swirling wind grabbed everything not tied down and blew it in out faces. The plane tipped further to the left, and I started slipping off my seat. I had forgotten to re-attach my seat belt.

"Help! I'm falling!" I screamed.

"Dan, hold on." Maria let go of the yoke and grabbed my jacket. That just made it worse. The plane tipped at a forty-five-degree angle.

Maria pulled with both hands. The airplane continued its dive. The wind wound a white bra around my head. I couldn't see anything.

"Grab the bra!" I yelled.

Maria pulled. The undergarment held and provided the needed leverage for me to regain my seat. We finally leveled off just feet above the waves.

"Are you okay," Maria asked.

"I guess so."

"Now what?"

"We'll try again."

The plane was a mess. The wind blew all my paper and much of Maria's laundry around the cabin.

"Did anything blow out while the door was open?" I asked.

"Just some papers. I wasn't paying attention."

I recovered my breath and said, "Thanks for saving my life."

"I owed you that. Besides, I'm getting to like you." She smiled and kissed me on the cheek.

We tried again. This time I used my seatbelt. Bit by bit Maria handed me the contents of our two suitcases followed by the suitcases themselves. Finally, she gave me a plastic bag, one that I assumed was full of trash. Only the bag of cocaine and my laptop retained their privileged positions on the back seat.

I locked the door and did one more circle so we could admire our handiwork. Maria's empty suitcase bobbed in the waves next to my khaki slacks. Nearby, a multicolored panty selection floated a few feet away from white jockey shorts. *Maybe they'll intertwine somewhere in the depths.*

"That's good enough to convince anyone," I said.

"I hope you're right. I have nothing to wear."

"I'll buy you new underwear in New York."

"What a gentleman!"

I turned off the transponder to complete our deception. Somewhere in a windowless ATC building, a controller noted the time the signal went out.

I brought the plane back to five hundred feet and turned west.

Chapter 19

Dan and Maria Make Plans

"The only time you have too much fuel," my flight instructor once told me, "is when your plane's on fire." I didn't have too much fuel. We could stay in the air only two more hours. Since we were heading into the wind, our flight back to land would take longer and use more fuel than our trip out to sea.

I visualized an ever-shrinking circle symbolizing the limit of our flight superimposed on a map of the Eastern United States. We had to find a place to land somewhere within that circle.

"Hungry?" Maria asked, interrupting my calculations.

"Yeah, what's on the menu?"

"We have a delightful assortment of protein bars, bologna sandwiches, and water."

"Stewardess, I could have sworn I reserved a first class seat."

"I'm sorry sir; this is definitely an economy flight. What do you want? I haven't got all day."

"I'll take a water and a protein bar." Maria opted for a sandwich.

The miles clicked slowly by. The fuel gauges moved unperceptively, from right to left. The watery landscape didn't change. "When do we get to LaGuardia?" Maria asked as she ate.

I laughed. "We can't land at LaGuardia."

"Don't laugh at me, big shot. Why can't we?"

"First off, small planes can't land there. More importantly, we dead now, remember? We can't land at any public airport. Someone will see my tail number and report us."

"So what are we going to do, Mr. Genius? We can't stay up here forever. Besides, I have to pee."

"My friend, Pete Swanson, owns a small farm with a private landing strip. There's a barn where we can hide the plane."

"Can we stay there?"

"Yeah, he's not there. He had a stroke last year and moved to Florida. I visited right before he moved and he showed me where he keeps a spare key. The farm is between Gettysburg and Harrisburg, Pennsylvania."

"You sure you can land there?"

"Landing on grass strips is my specialty."

"Okay, we land there, then what?"

"We'll stay the night. Tomorrow we'll borrow Pete's pickup truck and drive to New York."

"Sounds good, Dan. You're finally putting that brain to good use."

"Thanks, I guess. We have just enough fuel to get there as long as we don't do anything crazy along the way."

"Gotcha. No aerobatics."

We were halfway to land and about two hours away from Pete's farm. Once we got to land, I planned to stay away from radar-equipped airports. Our biggest danger was cell phone towers and other aircraft. As long as we stayed under the clouds, we would be okay.

The last time Pete and I were together, he wrote his farm's latitude and longitude on one of my sectional charts. "Just look for a long, narrow lake," he said. "My farm's at the north end of the lake. Call ahead, and I'll put on the coffee." I never had the chance to take him up on his offer.

"Maria, there's a plastic bag in the back with all my maps.

Please look through them, find the one titled *New York*, and hand it to me."

I kept my eyes straight ahead while she looked in the back. We were still forty-five minutes from land.

"What does the bag look like?" she asked.

"It's a white, plastic, grocery-store bag. You'll see a bunch of paper maps in it. It might have slipped under my seat."

She unfastened her seatbelt and got on her knees to search the back seat. "It's not here. I don't see it."

My heartbeat quickened. Sweat started to drip from my baseball cap. Without those numbers, we were lost.

"It has to be! Look again."

She leaned further into the back. I adjusted the trim to compensate for the weight change.

"Dan, I don't see a white, plastic bag. I don't see any plastic bags. Are you sure you had it?"

"Maria, Maria ... "

"Stop saying my name." She returned to her seat. "Your God damn maps aren't in the back seat."

"They have to be. We can't find Pete's farm without the chart."

"You look. I think you threw them out ... "

"If I threw them out, it was only because you handed them to me."

"I thought it was trash."

"God damn it, woman! Where's your head!"

"Fuck you!"

"Fuck you!"

"I'll look. Hold the plane."

I adjusted the trim while Maria put her hands on the yoke. I took off my headset so I could more easily maneuver. I looked under the passenger seat. No maps. I looked under my seat. No maps. The trickle of sweat turned into a stream. The maps were gone. I would have to fly the way it was done before electronics using dead reckoning and landmarks.

I regained my seat, put on my headset and took over the controls. A deep scowl covered my face. The smell of my worry overcame the stink from Maria's cigarettes.

"What are we gonna do?"

"I'll use my GPS as long as I can. Pete's farm is at the north end of a long, narrow lake. Once we find the lake, we'll find the landing strip."

"You're telling me we have to find a lake in Pennsylvania? Have you ever been there?"

"Yes, once, but I came by car."

"What if we can't find the lake in time?"

"We'll find the lake. How hard can it be?"

"We're fucked."

"Thanks for the moral support!"

I entered the code for the Gettysburg Airport into the GPS and adjusted our heading accordingly. I had to turn further into the wind to track our heading — more fuel to cover the same distance.

Maria finished a bottle of water and threw it in the back. She had a pensive, look on her face. "Dan, I don't mean to bother you while you're doing such a good job with this flying jalopy, but darling, *querido,* where did you put your money?"

"What money?"

"The money we split last night. I gave you five thousand dollars in hundred-dollar bills. I have mine in my purse." She held up her purse for me to see. "Where in this flying shithouse did you put yours?"

My heart sank. I knew what was coming next. "I put it in the zippered compartment of my suitcase. You have it don't you?"

"What do you mean?"

"Didn't you take the money from the suitcase before you

handed it to me?" My heart raced. It wasn't hard to anticipate her reaction.

"No, asshole, I didn't. Don't try to put this on me. It was your suitcase. You didn't tell me anything. You threw it out, and now it's a home for some fish."

I held my breath.

"You fucking idiot! *We* didn't get rid of the suitcase, *you* did! You told me to hand it to you. You threw five-thousand dollars into the waves!" She hit me in the back of the head three times.

"How the hell did I end up with you?" she shouted.

I wanted to say, you came running to me. I wanted to remind her that I kept her from becoming a bloodstain on the asphalt. Those words passed through my mind. A decade of marriage taught me to keep my mouth shut.

"Do you have any money left?" she asked in a calmer voice.

"About a thousand."

"Give it to me! If you hold onto it, it'll get swallowed by a whale." I handed her my wallet. She stuffed all but a few small bills into her bra. She saw me looking and said, "Keep your eyes on the road, pervert."

The flying pervert kept his eyes on the horizon. He concentrated on staying in the air between two bodies of water — liquid below, clouds above. If they hit an air pocket, the pervert and his companion would be in the wet before they knew it.

"I can't talk to you anymore," Maria sneered. She took off her headset and threw it on the floor, cutting off all communication. She stared out the right side window, her arms firmly locked across her chest. I stared straight ahead.

Fine, let her stew in her own juice. I'm tired of being bossed around.

Without my girlfriend's distractions, my heartbeat found the engine's rhythms, and I entered that special, mental space where

I became one with my airplane — yoke and rudder, no radio, no map — just me, the engine, the airplane and the endless sky. I had no past, no future, just a continuous present. Check heading. Check altitude. Check engine temperature. Repeat, repeat, again and again.

***

She hit me.

"Maria," I said without looking, "Please stop hitting me." She hit me again.

Her mouth moved, but without her headset, I had no idea what she was saying. She pointed. I realized words weren't necessary.

A great steel wall came towards us at incredible speed. It blocked out the sunlight. An apocalyptic destroyer, it obliterated everything in its path.

More than twenty stories high, the massive container ship sailed directly in our path.

Flying over wasn't an option — I could never gain altitude fast enough. I had to beat it by passing in front.

I added power and turned sharply to the left. I reduced altitude to gain speed, bringing my left wing dangerously close to the waves. I expected to hear the ship's horn blast a warning.

"Faster, *Chico!* You need to go faster!" She had her headset on again.

Maximum engine RPMs. Tipped at a forty-five-degree angle, pressed against our seatbelts, we waited for disaster. Maria grabbed my hand. She watched the ship. I watched the waves. We held our breaths. We screamed.

The enormous ship not only parted the waves, but it also pushed the air ahead of it. A great gust of air grabbed my light plane pushed it away from the bow. The great ship passed behind us. No horn blast. No contact.

"*Dios mio*, does that always happen when you fly, or only when I'm with you?"

I couldn't answer immediately. My hands were shaking. I brought the plane back to 500 feet, and reduced RPMs to save fuel.

"It doesn't always happen. We were flying too low. Can you hold the plane? I need some water." I looked at the fuel gauges. The high-RPM maneuver cost us. It was going to be tight.

I drank. She held the controls. The GPS informed me we were close to land.

"Maria, we would've died if you hadn't spotted the ship."

"I guess I saved your life. Now we're even."

***

Near Gettysburg, the solid clouds dissolved. We flew in partial sunlight. We'd been flying for more than four hours. Both fuel gauges registered less than an eighth of a tank. The GPS was useless. We needed to find Pete's landing strip as soon as possible.

"Maria, start looking for Pete's lake. It'll be long and narrow with trees on both sides. There's a clearing at the north end. You'll see a house and barn."

"I see lots of fields but no lakes."

Below us, Amish children waved as we flew over their neat farms. *Would any of them remember my tail number? Did it still matter?*

The land rose to meet us as we entered the Allegheny foothills. Rivers and forests replaced the farms. We had to be getting close.

The fuel gauges hovered over "E." We only had minutes left to fly.

"Maria, what do you see?"

"I see a lake. It's long and narrow."

"Where? Where's the lake."

"Over there, to my right."

It wasn't the right lake. There was no farm, no landing strip at the north end.

The engine coughed. I adjusted the mixture, reducing the fuel, adding more air. *Should we go on? Maybe it's just over the next hill?*

The engine hesitated again. Then it hit me — the plane had to die.

The plane had to die so we could live. I lost everything else. Now I'll lose my airplane, my aluminum mistress. It was the final plan.

The engine sputtered its agreement — it wanted to die. I wobbled the wings to drain the last pints of fuel. It came back to life, willing to give its last energy to support me.

"We're going to ditch the plane in the lake," I shouted. "We'll get to New York somehow. Take off your headset. I'll land as close to the middle of the lake as possible so when the plane sinks it will go all the way to the bottom. No one will ever find it."

"Are you fucking kidding me? You're gonna crash in the lake?"

"I'm not kidding. If I do it right, we'll land gently and swim to shore." A horrible thought entered my mind. "You can swim, can't you?"

"Yes, you fucking gringo, I can swim. I grew up on an island, remember?" After a pause, "You've done this before?"

"Hell no!"

"Madre de Dios."

The lake was about three miles long and a half-mile wide. I aligned our flight path with the lake's length, pretending it was a runway. The engine died a final time. No more fuel. The overwhelming engine noise was replaced by the quiet whisper of the wind. I unplugged my headset and threw it in the back. Maria tried to do the same, but her legs were tangled in the wires. I couldn't help her.

Fighting a cross wind, I gained speed by lowering the nose and turned towards the lake. "We're going to make it," I shouted. We crossed the last of the trees and flew over a small house. "Unbuckle your seatbelt!"

We were a few dozen feet above the water. I corrected to the right.

Too much.

All hell broke loose.

The right wing tip dug into the water. The plane cartwheeled. The momentum threw me against the unlocked door. A bolt of pain shot through my left shoulder, and the door flew open.

I got my left foot out, ready to jump. The door slammed shut on my calf. I heard a sharp crack. White hot pain radiated throughout my body.

The plane rotated on its wing, and the centrifugal force threw me out of the plane and into the air. Before I hit the water, I caught sight of my plane standing on its nose, balancing like an Olympic athlete. I never saw the end of its act.

I sank into the cold, dark water. *Which way's up?* My shoulder hurt. My leg hurt. My lungs hurt. I stroked with my right arm towards the less dark, the less cold.

Onto the surface. I had enough time to get a lungful of air before my waterlogged clothes dragged me under again.

I once took a course on how to ditch a plane and survive. "Take off your pants. Tie knots at the ends. Trap air inside. Use your pants as a life preserver." I knew what I had to do, but I couldn't move my left arm or bend my left leg.

Which way to land? Where's Maria?

I picked a direction. Tried to swim with one arm. Sank.

Did I remember to kick off my shoes? How will I get to New York without shoes?

One more stroke. One more gasp. One more. *Maybe I'm swimming down the spine of the lake, not to the nearest shore?* I looked around and just saw trees.

I need to get to shore. "Maria," I shouted. No reply.

Oh, my God. Did Maria get out of the plane? Is she dead? Did I kill her? "Mari…" I swallowed water and went down.

Why am I fighting? It's peaceful and dark down here. No responsibilities. Die for real. Maybe it's the best thing. Surrender to the cold and dark. I'll die with my airplane. One more stroke. *Just one more stroke.*

I sank. The lake became the YMCA pool. I was twelve years old. Mom told me not to dive off the high board, but the other boys called me a sissy. I dived. My head hit bottom. Blood in the water.

My mother's voice: *"I told you not to jump off the high board. Now you hurt your leg and your shoulder. I'm calling the lifeguard."*

"No mom, don't call the lifeguard. The other boys will make fun of me. It's okay. The cold and the dark are my friends."

"Turn over! Turn onto your back!" *Oh, man, Mom called the lifeguard.*

"Turn over, God damn it. *Chico,* turnover!"

The word "*Chico*" brought me back. I grabbed a lungful of air.

"Turn on your back, dumbass. How can you be so stupid? "

Maria's alive! I said goodbye to the cold and the dark and turned onto my back. Stroke by stroke, she pulled me towards a grassy bank.

"Can you stand?" she asked when we were in the shallows.

I tested my knees on the gravel. "No, my leg hurts too much." She helped me crawl out of the water.

"I'm pretty sure your leg's broke."

What had once been my calf was now an ugly, purple and

swelling object. Maria used my belt and a stick to fashion a crude splint.

"Your plane's still floating," she said. "Didn't you say it would sink?"

I looked toward the lake. My faithful plane lay upside down, immodestly displaying its landing gear. "The empty fuel tanks are holding it up. Don't worry, they'll soon fill with water, and it'll sink. No one will know that we landed here." I waited until my heart stopped pounding.

"I was drowning. I had given up. You saved my life. Again."

Maria grunted, pulling little twigs and leaves from her tangled hair. "I guess it's what we do. Save each other. One hell of a relationship."

"I need to get to a hospital. My leg hurts real bad."

"No joke. I think you hurt your side as well."

"Did you see any houses near the lake?"

"I think I saw one."

"Leave me here. Find the house. Tell them we had a car accident. Tell them our car crashed into the lake. Have them call 911. You go to New York, I'll join you when I get better. It will all work out. I'll learn Spanish. I'll find a job. Maybe we'll start a family, you and me? What do you ... "

A wave of pain. I passed out.

She slapped my face. "Dan, wake up! You were raving." She shook me.

"I guess I did. Don't worry, I have a plan. I've figured it all out."

"You and your fucking plans. You always have a plan. Half our cash went into the ocean because of your last plan."

"No, that was ... "

"Forget about it. Just stay here. Go back to sleep."

She stood up and took off her shoes, jeans, and t-shirt. The folded and placed them on top of a large rock. She transferred the wad of wet hundred dollar bills from her bra to her pant's pocket.

"Your clothes will never dry. It's too cloudy. Just go to … "

She ignored me and entered the lake in her underwear.

"Maria, what are you doing? Where are you going?"

She didn't answer. "Maria, where you going?"

She turned when the water was over her chest. "Just stay there, *Chico*. I need to get something."

"No, stop, it's too dangerous!"

The cocaine. She's risking her life for cocaine.

"Forget about the coke! Come back!" Each word hurt like a dagger's stab in my side.

She swam to the plane and held onto a wing while she caught her breath. She dove into the cabin. The wings shifted. She came back up on the other side and threw her purse onto the wing. She took a deep breath then dove down a second time.

A large burp came out of the back of the plane followed by a cloud of air bubbles. The tail sank. The nose bobbed up. The right wing dipped. The left wing came up. More burps. More bubbles. Quietly, the plane slipped below the surface and disappeared.

Chapter 20

Where's Maria?

She didn't come up. Why didn't she come up?

"Maria!"

A dozen mallards took flight from the opposite bank. No answer.

"Maria, I need you!" No response, not even from the waterfowl.

It was hard to breathe. *Did she drown? Did she die on the bank of this God-forsaken lake?*

Two rolls to the right brought me closer to the water, next to a small tree. I used the tree to painfully pull myself up. The surface of the lake lay undisturbed. No oil slick, no bubbles marked the place where my pride and joy slid beneath the surface.

I scanned left and right for my companion. At first, I looked for a strong swimmer, then for a floating body. I found nothing. The lakeside animals discussed the drama in a chorus of chirps, croaks, and twitters.

Maybe if I got closer...

I tried a quick hop towards a sapling closer to the water. Something moved in the bushes to my left — a flash of brown. I turned to look and lost my balance. My head hit a rock. The world went black.

Naked, Maria came out of the water like Venus in Botticelli's painting. The black duffle hung from her shoulder. "Come, Chico, we need to get going." She sat on ~~on~~ the rock and put on her clothes.

A long, black, limousine appeared just a few steps away. Richard, wearing a chauffeur's uniform, held the open door. "Daniel, me friend, so good to see you again. Get in. Relax, mon."

"I thought you were dead."

"Lot's of tings ain't wot dey seem. Get in, me friend."

I lay on my back with my head on Maria's lap. She smiled, with that special mischievous smile of hers and said, "You see, Dan, I told you it would be OK. I had a plan all along. Go to sleep."

We kissed. Her kisses had an earthy, salty taste. *When did she get such a long tongue?* I tried to return the kisses, but her hair kept getting in the way.

"Down girl, sit."

No one could talk to my girlfriend that way. I held my breath, anticipating the flood of vulgar Spanish. Whoever told Maria to sit would be very sorry. The kisses stopped. The curses never came.

My wet clothes absorbed all my body heat. "Richard, please turn up the heat, it's cold back here."

Richard didn't respond.

"You okay?"

I forced one eye open. Richard, Maria, and the limo were all gone. I felt the cold, wet, mud on my back.

I turned in the direction of labored panting and found a large golden retriever sitting obediently by my head.

I opened the other eye. The sun hung lower in the sky. *How long was I out?* The dog wagged its tail and raised one paw.

"Mister, were you in that plane?"

The words came from a tall white-haired man, well into his sixties. He was dressed in jeans and suspenders. Under the suspenders, he wore a red-checked work shirt. His nicotine-stained hand held the other end of a leash.

"Who are you? Where'd you come from?" I asked.

"Well, my name's not Richard and there ain't nothin' I can do about the heat," he responded with a chuckle. He examined me like I was a rare fossil. I listened to the birds while he considered his next statement.

"The name's Jake Smith," he continued. "I live at the other end of the lake. Your plane went right over my house. My dog Ruby, and me, we were out birding and saw the whole thing. We would've come sooner, but we had to walk around from the other side, and there are parts where there ain't no paths close to the water. You okay?" he asked again. I wanted to explain that I wasn't okay, but he wasn't finished. "Actually, your leg doesn't look too good. Your head either. You're bleeding at both ends."

"I guess I fell. Did you see my plane go down?

"Sure did. The bottom's no more than eighty feet deep. The divers won't have too much trouble pulling it out. Don't worry — I called the police when we saw you crash. Then I called the EMT when I saw you swim to the bank. There's a road about a thousand yards away. The EMT boys should be here soon."

"Did you see a woman swimming in the lake?"

He laughed again, and that really upset me. "No, I didn't. People don't go swimming in the lake. Too cold. We use it mostly for fishing. Was she with you?"

"Yes, she was. Are you certain you didn't see anyone? She might be mostly naked."

"Well, in that case, I sure would've noticed. Nope, didn't see nobody, naked or dressed, 'cept you, of course. You know, mister, it looks like you did hit your head real bad and — "

I dismissed his medical opinion. "Name's Maria. About five-foot-five, long black hair. Those are her clothes over there. Don't let your dog mess with her clothes."

I pointed to the rock. We both looked. It stared back in naked reproach.

"There ain't nothin' on that rock but moss and lichen. Ain't seen no woman, naked or otherwise. Why'd she go swimmin' anyway?"

"She went back to get something from the plane before it sank."

"So you're saying that there's a naked woman swimming around in my lake?"

Damn fool!

"If her clothes are gone, she's not naked anymore. She must have come out, while I was unconscious."

"You sure?"

At least she's not drowned.

"She might be hiding in the woods."

"Or maybe you just hit your head. I think you need to calm down."

"Maria! Maria, come here," I shouted.

Her name echoed off the surrounding hills. No response. I called again. The echoes repeated her name, again and again, each time more faintly. My side hurt. I couldn't take a deep breath. My eyes began to lose focus.

"You better relax, son," my savior advised a second time. "You really did a number on that leg. We need to get you to a hospital."

It had been a long time since anyone called me son. I would have smiled, but with every passing second, the adrenaline masking my pain began to wear off. Between the waves of agony came the growing realization — Maria's gone.

That bitch. She swam to the plane, retrieved the drugs, got dressed and walked away while I lay unconscious in the mud. She'll sell the drugs and set up a new life in New York or wherever. No note. No "Dear John" letter. Maybe that's what I was to her after all — one of her many "Johns."

A tear started down my face.

"That's okay, son. If you need to cry, just cry. Let me help with the leg." He bent down and tried to straighten my leg. Whatever pain I had felt before paled in comparison to the white-hot overwhelming lighten bolt coursing through my body. I screamed so loud the dog hid behind the rock.

The screams paid off. Male voices responded.

Smith shouted, "Over here, over here by the lake." Minutes later, four uniformed men emerged from the woods carrying an aluminum stretcher.

"Where are we?" I asked. I tried to address one of the paramedics, but Smith wasn't ready to relinquish his role as rescuer-in-chief.

"Well sir, we call this Edgewood Lake. These boys are from the Shamokin Fire Department. Shamokin, that's the nearest town. They got a nice hospital there. If they can't help you in Shamokin, they'll take you to Harrisburg."

The lead paramedic shined a light in my eyes. "What's your name?"

"Dan Goldberg."

"How many fingers do you see?"

"Two."

"What's the day of the week?"

"Saturday." Unbelievably, I left my home only five days before.

"Are you allergic to any medicines?"

"No."

"Good, we'll give you something for the pain."

They carried me across several small streams and endless rocks on the way to the ambulance. Each step brought another wave of pain. I passed out again.

I woke in the hospital's emergency room. Two nurses held

me down while a doctor dressed my put an inflatable cast on my leg. Something in the IV drip kept most of the pain at bay.

The lady from the admissions office stopped by to confirm my address and insurance information. "Who would you like us to call?" she asked. "We already called your wife. We found your emergency contact information in your wallet."

"What did she say?"

She hesitated. "I don't want to upset you."

"What did she say," I asked again, my voice rising.

"Well, she took the information about you and about our hospital."

"Is she coming to see me?"

"She's not sure. She thought you died."

After she had left, I looked through my wallet. My credit cards and the few dollars Maria hadn't confiscated were all there. The side compartments held my driver's license and medical insurance cards. I pulled everything out and searched again, this time more frantically.

Where is it?

I couldn't find the one item I really wanted — Richard's business card, the one with his sister's phone number.

Chapter 21

Dan's Decision

I couldn't sleep. Every time I dozed, someone would fiddle with a tube or wire attached to my body. The next day, Sunday was much of the same. The nurse explained that they only handled emergencies surgeries on weekends and my broken leg didn't qualify. Towards evening, they taught me how to use the button managing my pain medicine, and I finally fell into a deep sleep.

I stood on the porch of a small beach house. The smell of jasmine signaled Jamaica. A woman came towards me walking along the waterline. She had Maria's black hair and wore the same style swimsuit. My heart skipped a beat. Could it be?

"Maria, you're here?"

"*Sí*, I here."

Cautiously, I opened my eyes. The gray light of dawn filtered into the room. A middle-aged woman, shorter and at least seventy-five pounds heavier than my girlfriend leaned over my bed with a mop in her right hand.

"You're not Maria."

"*Sí*, me name Maria." After a moment she continued, "I come clean the room. I wake you?"

She turned on the overhead light and showed me her ID badge with her name, Maria Ortez, in bold letters.

"I'm sorry. I guess I was dreaming. *"*

"It okay. I go now."

***

I was just recovering from the surprise when a doctor breezed in followed by a half-dozen white-coated students.

"Good morning mister, Goldberg. I'm Dr. Choudhary, your orthopedic surgeon. Let's see what we have here."

I was about to tell him, but one of the acolytes signaled me to be quiet as he clipped three x-rays photos to the light box on the wall. "Very interesting, how did you manage to do that?"

"My airplane crashed into a lake not far from here. The door slammed —"

"You're a pilot?"

"I am … I was. I think my piloting days are over."

"It says here you cracked two ribs and smashed your left calf.

Speaking to the students, he said, "The patient's left calf presents with a broken bone. Luckily, the ends didn't break the skin." He consulted my chart again. "He also had a minor concussion, but we'll let the head guys handle that." It was his idea of a joke, and the entourage giggled.

The doctor turned to me. "We've scheduled you for surgery tomorrow morning. When we're done, you'll have screws in your leg for the rest of your life. After surgery, you'll stay here a few days, then transfer to a rehabilitation facility. You'll need to stay off the leg for at least four weeks."

"Do you know what happened to my passenger?"

He scowled at the interruption. "As far as I know, you were the only survivor." He wrote a few words on my chart and signed the bottom of the page with a flourish. The group left in a white snowstorm. Moments later a harried nurse came in with an armful of forms.

I wanted to leave Maria a voice mail message, but couldn't remember her phone number. My voice mailbox had many messages — none from Maria.

Beth's came first. "Don't come home, you indescribable bastard. If you wanted to have an affair, why couldn't you have a simple, discreet one like all the other philandering jerks in the neighborhood? You had to take it extremes and have it plastered all over the news. I'm so embarrassed. Go to hell!"

The police and FAA officials left messages demanding return calls. The final message came from a prospective client offering a long-term contract. He obviously had not been watching the news.

The nurses gave me a pill, and I slept the rest of the day and night.

The operating room staff woke me at dawn the next day, Tuesday, and wheeled me away. Four or five people worked around me attaching wires and tubes. When all was ready, the anesthesiologist told me to count down from one hundred. I got to ninety-two.

I awoke in the cold, dark recovery room. A heavy, plaster cast encased my leg from groin to toes. I hurt all over.

A woman sat in the chair next to my bed. "Maria?"

"No, asshole, it's your wife. Sorry to disappoint."

"Beth, you came! I didn't think you'd come. Thank you." Tears rolled down my cheeks.

"You're welcome. I came only because Sara insisted. Maybe I shouldn't have. Does your leg hurt?"

"Yeah, real bad."

"Good. Maybe you can appreciate what I've been through." A nurse came in and asked me to count her fingers. She did something with one of the tubes. I nodded off.

The next time I opened my eyes, I was back in my room. Beth sat in a chair by the window.

"Beth?"

"Congratulations, you got it right this time."

"Are the girls here?"

"No, I came alone. The surgeon said the operation was successful. They put a dozen screws in your leg. The doctor says with physical therapy, you'll be able to walk again. Your flying days are over. Not because of your broken leg, but because of your horrible behavior. The FAA's coming tomorrow. I get all your messages. Everyone treats me like I'm still your wife."

"Aren't you?"

"Maybe. We'll talk again when you have a clearer head. As far as I'm concerned, we're not married anymore. I need to leave. I'll be back on Friday." She put her purse down and came close to the head of my bed.

"You took me on quite a ride. You hardly talk to me all week, a week when your daughter was in the hospital. Finally, on Friday, you tell me to buy steaks. You said you were coming home early with a new contract. But you never came home. The girls saw you on TV with another woman! Our friends saw you. My parents! Can you imagine how I felt?"

"I'm sorry."

"Fuck you and your sympathy. The only bright spot came Saturday. When I heard you crashed at sea. I got to be the grieving widow for four or five hours. Then I found out you're not dead — just half-downed in Pennsylvania. You couldn't even die right!"

She walked to the window and looked out. She blew her nose using tissue from the box by my bedside.

"How could you be so stupid?"

"I wasn't stupid. It started out when I gave a friend a ride and then —"

"I don't want to hear about it." She picked up her purse again.

I closed my eyes, hoping she'd take the hint and leave. Instead, she shook the bed. "Who's the woman?" she demanded.

I opened my eyes. "Her name's Maria Sanchez. I saved her

life on Friday. She saved me from drowning on Saturday. Did they find her body?"

One of the machines near the head of my bed started to beep. A nurse walked in and adjusted something.

After the nurse had left, Beth said, "No one told me anything about a body."

"Maybe she got away."

"You still didn't tell me who she was." She closed the door to the hallway and lowered her voice. "Did you have sex with her?"

"Yes, at first it was a kind of accident ..."

"Bullshit! Stubbing your toe is an accident. Crashing your car is an accident. Did you have an *accidental* erection?"

"I was drunk and — "

"Shut up, I don't want to hear about it." She raised her hand, but the slap never came. "I'd slap you if I thought it would do any good."

She paced back and forth, holding up her hand as a signal for me to stay quiet.

"One question, then I'll leave. Do you love me?"

"Yes."

"Do you love your children?"

"Yes."

"Do you love her, your Maria?

"Yes."

"You fucking idiot! You think you can have us all, don't you? Grow up, Dan. It doesn't work that way."

I said nothing. She was right. Maybe some men could do it, not me. I suddenly realized that was the big lie I was telling myself.

"I'll be back on Thursday. We'll have a lot to talk about." She left.

***

I spent the rest of the day napping and watching television. I called my voice mailbox several times in the vain hope Maria left a message.

I know she's alive. She'll contact me soon enough.

Representatives from the FAA and the Pennsylvania State Police arrived after breakfast the next day. The man from the FAA spoke first. "We diverted some scheduled flights and grounded others so you wouldn't hurt anyone besides yourself. You created air traffic delays throughout the entire eastern part of the United States. Thousands of passengers were inconvenienced."

"Sorry," I said trying to insert a mournful tone into my voice.

His face turned red. "We revoked your pilot's license yesterday. You'll never fly again, in the United States. Expect a hefty fine." He gave me some official looking papers and left.

The state trooper closed the door after his colleague. "That man needs to calm down, or he'll have a heart attack." He put a small recorder on my bedside table. "Why don't you tell me what happened. Start with Ms. Sanchez. How do you know her?"

"I met Maria at the hotel, last Monday. We had an affair starting on Wednesday. I thought it had ended, but she stopped me just when I was about to fly home and begged me to take her with me."

"That was last Friday at the Gaithersburg airport, right?"

"Right. We spent the night in Cumberland, Maryland and were on our way to New York, when the FAA ordered us to land. Instead, we headed out to sea and dumped our luggage to make it look like we crashed. On the return, we ran out of fuel before I could find a safe place to land."

The lieutenant took notes during most of my rendition. "We've checked with the authorities in Cumberland, and they confirmed you and Ms. Sanchez landed there. We know that you spent the night at the Hilltop Motel using aliases." He smirked, "John Katz and June Satin, really?"

"Seemed like a good idea at the time."

He shook his head. "The airport manager said you were the only person he saw when you returned the loaner car on Saturday. Later that day he reported the car missing. The police found the car in the long-term parking lot at the Pittsburgh International Airport late Sunday night."

The Lieutenant paused. "Do you have anything to add?"

"It must be a coincidence."

"The FBI will be here to talk to you next. Don't run away," he added with a chuckle.

More comedy, just what I needed.

He left as the lunch tray came in. I couldn't eat. The life I'd built and nurtured during my adult years was over. After the heartache, training, and sacrifice, I no longer had a pilot's license. My marriage was all but over. I was heading to prison.

Out of the emptiness came a certain sense of relief. All these identities that defined me — pilot, husband, father, professor — were like weights around my neck. I could feel them dropping away, one by one, like a snake shedding its skin. I felt scared, vulnerable and, in a weird way — free.

Janice Joplin once sang, "Freedom's just another word for nothing left to lose." I felt myself moving closer and closer to nothing.

***

Three FBI agents, two men, and a woman entered my room at the end of the day.

"Daniel Goldberg, you are under arrest for intentionally violating restricted airspace, reckless endangerment, disobeying ATC orders and flying an airplane without the use of proper equipment. The charges are detailed in these papers."

"Do you wish to make a statement?" the lead agent asked.

"No. I already gave a statement to the State Trooper."

"We would like to ask you some questions, but first I need to read this."

He read the Miranda warnings from a card. I recited the same story I told the state trooper. I never mentioned Richard or the flight to New Jersey.

They ended the interview after an hour, suggesting I get a lawyer.

***

On Thursday, Beth walked dressed in a black suit, white silk blouse, and pantyhose. I could tell that she had a prepared speech.

"Good morning, Dan. Here's how we can put this behind us. You had a stupid obsession with flying, but that's over. Your airplane's sitting at the bottom of a lake. You'll never be a pilot again. You had a stupid affair —." She stopped to wipe away a tear.

"Beth, I'm sorry — "

"Don't interrupt me! Damn it, I promised myself I wouldn't cry."

I handed her the box of tissues.

"Okay, you humiliated me. I can handle that. Here's what I'm trying to say — I'm willing to put your affair behind me for the sake of our children."

Tears covered her face. She went into the bathroom and returned even angrier.

"My father thinks you'll be in prison for at least three years. I want to put our house on the market and move closer to my parents. I need you sign the listing forms." She handed me a stack of legal-sized papers from a new Coach briefcase.

"Nice briefcase."

She handed me a pen, and I added my signature on each page.

"Dad is buying me a small house in White Plains, about ten miles from where they live. The girls aren't happy about changing schools, but they'll adjust. Dad will take care of the girls and me financially until I get a job."

"Your father's a very generous man."

"He's doing it for his granddaughters. He's disgusted with me for putting up with you all these years. My mother pities me. You're an embarrassment to the family."

She took a sip of water from the cup on my nightstand.

"Dan, I can wait three years. I'll even visit you in prison once in a while. I'll put up with the dirty looks from my parents, relatives, and neighbors. But for that to work, you need to promise me you're done with your obsessions — all of them. You need to promise me that you're done with Maria or any other woman. Can you be a faithful husband, loving father, and respectful son-in-law?" She took a breath. "I need to know that you'll never do anything like this again."

It was my turn to talk. I knew that I should beg for forgiveness and say "yes." The next words out of my mouth would determine my future. Similar to the moment at the stoplight in Cumberland, I held my future in my hands.

I had to promise to be three things. Each one subtracted from the freedom I'd started to feel.

The week taught me there was more to me than my resume. Again and again, I pitted myself against the unknown and, in one way or another, I survived. I felt more alive during the previous week than I had ever felt before. I wasn't ready to give it up.

"I'm not the man you married."

"I know that. We all change as we get older."

"I'm not sure what kind of person I'll be when I get out of prison. I can't make the promises you want me to make. Actually,

I don't want to make them."

"Fuck you. Your Maria is dead or gone. What are telling me?"

"I can't make these promises. I'm a different person than I was last week."

"Fuck you and your hippy-dippy philosophy! Fuck you and your precious Maria. I'll be back tomorrow."

***

That night Richard came to me in my dream. *Hey, Daniel, my man. Dey treating you okay? Didn't I tell you dat woman be trouble? You take care of youself.*

I woke up in a cold sweat. *If only Maria would visit. Why didn't she call?*

Beth arrived Friday morning wearing her business suit and a new, short hairstyle.

"What's this?" She pulled an envelope from her purse. It was the one I sent on Saturday.

"It's a letter and a key to a safe deposit box."

"What's in the box?"

I lowered my voice, "Money, lots of money."

Beth adjusted her volume to match mine. "How much?"

"About $600,000. Enough to send both girls to college."

"Where did you get it?"

"Do you really want to know?"

She thought for a moment. "This has something to do with drugs and the Cartel you've been talking about, doesn't it?"

"Yes."

"I don't want to know, and I don't want the money. Take it." She pushed the envelope onto my chest.

"What about college?"

"It's not worth it. I don't know what you're involved in. I want no part of it."

"Beth, I'm — "

"What? You're sorry? It's too late for remorse. I asked you for three promises. Do you have anything more to say about that?"

"No."

"Goodbye, Dan. You'll hear from my attorney."

***

They moved me to a rehabilitation hospital the following week. A week after that, Beth's lawyer, an earnest young man, presented the divorce papers. That same week, deputies wheeled me into a courtroom. With the help of the lawyer from the public defender's office, I pleaded guilty. The judge sentenced me to six years at the Frostburg, Maryland minimum-security prison.

My lawyer told me I could get out in three years with good behavior. I looked forward to jail. I was destitute, homeless, and about to be incarcerated, but in my mind — I was free.

Epilog

Frostburg Federal Minimum Security Prison,
Frostburg, Maryland
August 1, Two years in prison

Two years have passed. My leg healed, and I walk the prison yard every day. On a good day, I can do a mile. Surprising to say, I'm enjoying my time in jail, and with good behavior, I'll be out in twelve months.

My companions are all white collar criminals. Each one has an interesting past. Each crossed the line separating right from wrong, legal from illegal at some point and they all had good, "higher" reasons for doing so. We talk about this in our group counseling sessions. The counselors want us to confront our mistakes and resolve to do better. We're all convinced our biggest mistake was getting caught.

I dream about my twin passions — flying and Maria. The two are inseparably linked. On some nights I can almost feel Maria sleeping beside me. On other nights, I'm back with Richard, flying in the rain.

When I'm outside, I listen for the sound of a single-engine plane, and when I hear one, my heart skips a beat.

My daughter Amy hasn't forgiven me and wants nothing to do with me. I wasn't there for her when she broke her arm. She never writes or visits. Sara comes when she can and writes often.

Recently, she told me Beth is dating a nice man, a lawyer. He's one of her father's associates. I'm happy for my ex-wife.

**

Two years, two months in prison

Another two months have passed. Ten months until my release. I have no idea of what I'll do when I get out.

**

Two years, five months in prison.
Seven months until my release.

Today everything changed. After breakfast, I went to my mailbox hoping for a letter from Sara. Instead, I found a picture postcard. The front of the card showed a beach scene with palm trees and a grass shack. It was a standard tourist postcard with the imprinted words, "Negril, Jamaica." On the back, I found the words, "Wish you were here," in a woman's handwriting. The letter "M" had pride of place below it.

Underneath the M were the words, "Relax Mon" in a man's heavy handwriting signed with the letter "R."

The End

(Maybe)

Howard Hammerman

Howard Hammerman grew up on a farm not far from New York City. His love of flying started, when, as a youngster, his father bought him a 15-minute ride on a bi-plane. Many years later he became a private pilot (instrument rated) and owned his own Cessna Cardinal. His fascination with people and the choices they make in their lives started in college Sociology courses. He taught college then became an analyst with the US government hoping to make a difference in the world.

He has been a freelance statistical consultant since 1990.

Howard, his artist-wife Helen and their dog traveled the country for several years in their motor home before settling in Sarasota, Florida, where they enjoy the support for creative arts of all types.

Flying Blind is his first novel.

A routine traffic stop ignites
a bloody mob vendetta...

The LAST GOODBYE

by GARY LOVISI

A "Vic Powers" mystery thriller,
plus three exciting short stories!

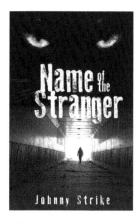

Made in the USA
Columbia, SC
02 October 2017